"I wish I could have a boy *and* a girl."

"I'm not volunteering again!" Kate laughed.

Tony grinned. "You sure?" Then he caressed her abdomen. "What a gorgeous sight. Every day you look more like a…"

"Beached whale?"

His chuckle rumbled through her. "I was going to say fertility goddess." He studied her intently. "I'm sorry I haven't been around more during the pregnancy. I hate having missed any part of it."

"Well, obviously, you had to miss the first part." Kate could tell from his heightened color that he was picturing it…and so was she.

She did her best to release the image, but the warmth of his hand remained pressed to her abdomen.

"What are you thinking?" he murmured.

"I wish we'd made her the old-fashioned way."

Dear Reader,

How can anyone not be fascinated by what happens when a woman promises to bear a baby for a childless couple? In what used to be a science fiction twist, today's reality often involves an infant whose DNA comes not from the surrogate but from the couple. But not always.

How does a woman feel about giving up a child who's genetically half hers? I'm a great believer in keeping promises, but as a novelist, I have to wonder what would happen if circumstances took an unexpected turn.

In the first book of the SAFE HARBOR MEDICAL miniseries, hospital attorney Tony Franco's wife, Esther, left him without warning. Off she went to a glamorous career in Washington, leaving confusion in her wake.

At the start of book two, surrogate Kate Evans has no idea that Esther's just dumped a dilemma in her rapidly vanishing lap. A widow with a five-year-old son, she's making plans for a future that doesn't include falling in love with her baby's father, or raising a daughter.

But the best laid plans have just gone astray, and thereby lies a tale. Happy reading!

Best wishes,

Jacqueline Diamond

His Hired Baby

JACQUELINE DIAMOND

TORONTO • NEW YORK • LONDON
AMSTERDAM • PARIS • SYDNEY • HAMBURG
STOCKHOLM • ATHENS • TOKYO • MILAN • MADRID
PRAGUE • WARSAW • BUDAPEST • AUCKLAND

Recycling programs
for this product may
not exist in your area.

ISBN-13: 978-0-373-75324-6

HIS HIRED BABY

ABOUT THE AUTHOR

Surrogacy and childbearing issues continue to fascinate Jacqueline Diamond even twenty years after her own two sons were born. A former Associated Press reporter and TV columnist, Jackie has sold more than eighty novels, and also teaches writing. You can learn more about her and her books at www.jacquelinediamond.com, and write to her at jdiamondfriends@yahoo.com.

Books by Jacqueline Diamond

HARLEQUIN AMERICAN ROMANCE

962—DIAGNOSIS: EXPECTING BOSS'S BABY
971—PRESCRIPTION: MARRY HER IMMEDIATELY
978—PROGNOSIS: A BABY? MAYBE
1046—THE BABY'S BODYGUARD
1075—THE BABY SCHEME
1094—THE POLICE CHIEF'S LADY*
1101—NINE-MONTH SURPRISE*
1109—A FAMILY AT LAST*
1118—DAD BY DEFAULT*
1130—THE DOCTOR + FOUR*
1149—THE DOCTOR'S LITTLE SECRET
1163—DADDY PROTECTOR
1177—TWIN SURPRISE
1209—THE FAMILY NEXT DOOR†
1223—BABY IN WAITING†
1242—MILLION-DOLLAR NANNY†
1273—DOCTOR DADDY
1295—THE WOULD-BE MOMMY**

*Downhome Doctors
†Harmony Circle
**Safe Harbor Medical

To my hardworking writing students

Chapter One

Doors had become a problem. Even the extra-wide entrance to the Safe Harbor Maternity Clinic scarcely looked big enough for Kate Evans to waddle through with her seven-month bulge.

She didn't recall having this much trouble getting in and out of cars or buildings during her first pregnancy, but five years ago she'd been only twenty-two. Everything had been easier then.

At the check-in desk, Kate waited behind a rail-thin young woman—perhaps one of the clinic's fertility patients—and a heavyset woman in her late thirties. Judging by the size of the older woman's midsection, she would probably precede Kate into the birthing unit at the medical center next door to the clinic.

Although giving birth to her son Brady had been the greatest thrill of her life, Kate wasn't looking forward to labor and delivery. Partly because of the pain, of course, but also because this time the doctor would be placing the baby in another woman's arms.

Even though Kate had chosen to do this of her own free will, that was going to hurt.

The line moved quickly. After signing her name and confirming her payment information, Kate headed for the elevator. She entered it right behind the heavyset woman, whom she vaguely recognized from previous visits.

"When are you due?" the woman asked as the doors closed, isolating the two of them.

"Mid-December." Kate marveled at the poor judgment of whoever had decided to line one wall of the elevator with a mirror. It showed her wispy brown hair, the slightly smudged makeup beneath her amber eyes, and the Jupiter-size swelling where her waist used to be. "You?"

"November. Next month," the woman added in amazement. "Gosh, I can't believe I'm nearly there. Three years of fertility treatments and now my baby's just a month away."

"Congratulations." To Kate's relief, the doors opened on the second floor. She preferred to avoid the baby-related conversations that naturally sprang up between expectant mothers.

Vain hope, she realized as the woman paced beside her along the hallway. "You see Dr. Rayburn too, don't you? I'm Rosemary, by the way."

"I'm Kate." She hoped her brisk tone would discourage further inquiry. Too bad, because under other circumstances Kate would have enjoyed getting to know this friendly mother-to-be.

"My husband couldn't take off work today," her companion continued. "He hates missing these appointments. I don't recall seeing your husband or significant other."

Kate rejected the usual white lie—"He travels a lot"—in favor of the truth. "Actually, he's dead."

"Oh!" Rosemary's mouth dropped open. "I'm sorry. How horrible for you that he died while you're pregnant."

"He died two years ago."

"He…what?"

At the office labeled Mark Rayburn, M.D., Kate eyed

the doorway dubiously. "I could swear that was wider last month."

"You have to pick your angle." Rosemary eased through. "Your husband left a sperm sample?"

Kate followed her inside. "No. I'm a surrogate."

"Oh. But how can you bear to…" Rosemary broke off. "It's none of my business, really." She headed for the counter.

Kate hung back, but her brain finished the sentence automatically. *How can you bear to give it up?* Also, *How can you carry someone else's baby?* She heard those questions often, along with the nosy, *How much are they paying you?* and the disdainful, *What kind of mother are you, anyway?*

The kind who wanted to help an infertile couple have a baby. The kind who, much as she'd have liked to do it for free, could certainly use the money to start her son's college fund and go back to school to become a nurse. Plus, in all honesty, she happened to be the kind of person who sometimes leaped before she looked.

Boy, had she leaped off this cliff, Kate conceded. She still didn't quite dare peek at the rapidly approaching ground below.

Yet by all reasonable measures, things were working out fine. Two months from now, a baby boy would get his chance at life and she could move on to build a future for herself and Brady.

After Rosemary sat down, Kate signed in. This clinic sure required a lot of paperwork, she reflected, but that seemed to be standard these days.

"You're here for an ultrasound?" the receptionist asked.

"Not that I'm aware of." In the office interior, Kate

glimpsed nurse Lori Ross's familiar freckled face. "Lori, what's this about an ultrasound?" she called.

The nurse's startled expression showed a hint of alarm, or was that Kate's imagination? "Dr. Rayburn thought it might be a good idea."

"Is something wrong?"

"No. Not at all." But there *was* a trace of anxiety in Lori's voice.

The nurse hurried away, leaving Kate to take a seat. Since there were only two other women in the room, she had no trouble finding a spot far from Rosemary, who was leafing through a parenting magazine.

Kate tried not to worry. Lori had a lot on her mind these days, what with planning her Christmas wedding to a handsome neonatologist. She was probably worried about some detail or other.

As she lowered herself onto the chair, Kate felt her abdomen ripple. At this stage, the baby was squeezed too tight for his earlier acrobatics, but she loved the reminder that there was a real little boy in there. Artie, she'd nicknamed him. His parents had chosen the name Arthur, after one of his grandfathers.

If only she could hold Artie in her arms and gaze into his cute face, Kate thought with a rush of longing. She pictured his tiny mouth working as he nursed, the way Brady's had. But she wasn't going to breastfeed this baby. She doubted Esther and Tony Franco would even want her to express milk for him, not that she blamed them. Once he emerged into the world, Artie would be their son, not hers.

Except that wasn't entirely true. Not only had she carried him for all these months, but he'd been conceived through artificial insemination using Kate's egg.

Initially, she'd intended to carry a baby that wasn't

genetically related. But she'd sympathized when she learned that Esther Franco had suffered premature ovarian failure in her early thirties.

Since then, doubts occasionally crept in, especially when Kate's sister Mary Beth began fuming about how unfair it was that she had to lose all contact with her future nephew. Well, the Francos—both attorneys—had insisted Kate sign a contract almost as long as the telephone book. Like it or not, she'd committed to giving up her baby.

For reassurance, she popped open her overstuffed purse and dug for her wallet. She needed to gaze at a photo of the precious little boy she already had.

Bad move. Out tumbled a toy car, a wad of receipts and a brochure from the California State University, Long Beach nursing program.

"Here. Let me." To her surprise, Rosemary trundled across the room and grabbed the toy car rolling across an adjacent chair. Had it made the plunge to the floor, neither of them could have retrieved it without help.

"Thanks," Kate said thickly, and hoped the other woman didn't notice the huskiness in her voice.

Rosemary handed her the toy and settled onto a neighboring seat. "You have other children?"

"My son's in kindergarten," Kate conceded, shoving everything into her purse. "You?"

A headshake. "My first." Rosemary drummed her fingers on her knee. "Do you mind my asking why you decided to do this?"

"I don't mind." Kate had answered that question often enough before. "While I could still stand on my feet all day, I worked at a beauty shop. One day between customers, I read a magazine article about a woman who carried a baby for another couple. It sounded so miraculous. Then my next client was a pediatrician, Dr. Forrest, who works at the hospital here, so I asked her opinion. Turned out she knew a couple who were desperate to have a baby, and, well, the whole thing seemed like destiny."

She didn't mention Tony Franco's position as staff attorney at the Safe Harbor Medical Center. He and Esther, a prosecutor with the Orange County District Attorney's office, had a right to decide for themselves how much to reveal to others about their new baby.

Nor did she care to admit that "desperate to have a baby" no longer fit the situation. Initially, Esther had seemed wild to become a mother and a friend, even inviting Kate to her house to suggest ideas for the nursery. Since then, however, either her interest had waned or she'd been overwhelmed by her workload. She hadn't joined Kate at checkups for months, leaving that task to her husband, who attended whenever some last-minute crisis didn't intervene.

On each occasion, Tony had asked concerned questions about Kate's care. Afterwards, he'd sent her gift certificates to her favorite store so she could buy treats for herself and Brady. Sometimes he seemed like the only parent who was truly involved.

Surely all that would change once Esther held the baby, though. Once she took the planned leave from her high-pressure job, there'd be plenty of time for mother and baby to bond.

Rosemary's next query was right on target. "Any second thoughts?"

Kate took a deep breath. "A few. I guess that's unavoidable, but this experience has been good for me. My husband died suddenly in an off-road vehicle accident, and I had trouble visualizing my future without him. This pregnancy has helped me move on. It's like getting a fresh start."

"That's beautiful." Rosemary might have said more, but

Lori appeared and called her name. "Thanks for putting up with my curiosity."

"No problem. It's only natural."

Once the other woman left, Kate restored her purse to order. Thank goodness the conversation had taken her mind off the unexpected ultrasound. Now, as she thought about it, her palms prickled, and she was glad Lori returned quickly to call her in.

"What's up?" she asked as the nurse weighed her.

"I'm sorry?"

"The ultrasound."

"Dr. Rayburn just wants to confirm something." Seeing a pucker form between the nurse's eyebrows, Kate got the impression she wanted to say more. Instead, Lori swiveled and led the way to a room with an ultrasound machine next to the examining table.

Usually, the nurse lingered to chat about her wedding plans since, in a small way, they involved Kate's baby. As Lori's best friend since high school, Esther was matron of honor, and the reception would be held at her and Tony's home overlooking the harbor. If Artie arrived on time, he'd be the tiniest guest at the event.

Today, however, the bride-to-be was all business. "You know the drill. Disrobe, put on the gown, push the green button to tell us you're ready."

"Tony isn't coming?" Kate asked.

"I think he's tied up."

Well, that wasn't unusual. "What about Esther?" she asked as Lori started for the door.

The nurse paused. "Excuse me?"

"Surely someone told her about the ultrasound."

"Well, no." Lori shifted from one foot to the other. "As a matter of fact, she's in Washington, D.C."

"Why?"

"At a conference or something. The doctor will be right in." She breezed off, leaving Kate more unsettled than ever.

Dr. Rayburn appeared soon afterwards. A powerfully built man with kind dark eyes, he served as hospital administrator in addition to seeing patients, yet he never seemed in a rush.

After asking how she felt—fine—and whether she'd encountered any problems—she hadn't—he instructed Kate to lie back for the ultrasound. "I thought I'd conduct this myself," he noted as he spread cool gel on her stomach.

"Why? Did you find some...?" She couldn't finish the sentence.

"Nothing to worry about." As he moved the small paddle across her stomach, images swirled on the monitor. "I was reviewing your file as a matter of routine, and I think the technician may have misinterpreted something."

Her throat tightened. "What?"

"Just a moment... There!" He examined the screen. "I was right. The technician confused an umbilical cord with a certain portion of the male anatomy. That is definitely a little girl."

Relief pumped through Kate. Was that all? "Oh, it's a she!" *Not Artie, but...* The name wasn't up to her. "Shouldn't the Francos be here for this?"

"Yes, they should." Dr. Rayburn tapped notes into a computer terminal. "It says here you haven't started your childbirth classes. If you wait any longer, you won't have time to finish."

"Esther's my birthing partner. She promised to set it up." And hadn't, obviously.

"There's a session starting tomorrow night." Dr. Rayburn regarded her thoughtfully. "I can sign you up now."

"Okay. Thanks." Watching him input the information,

Kate supposed she could ask her mother to accompany her. She'd need *someone* to be with her in the delivery room.

"Have you talked to either of the Francos this week?" the obstetrician asked.

"No." Although his position as hospital administrator made him Tony's boss, Dr. Rayburn was *her* doctor. Hesitantly, she said, "I'm not sure what's going on. This last month or so, I hardly hear from them."

"In this kind of situation, communication is essential," he said. "I'm going to call Tony's office and advise him that you're stopping by with some news. Or I can tell him about the gender myself if you'd prefer."

"No, I…I really need to get straight about who's going to be my birthing partner."

A few minutes later, Kate was en route to the hospital next door. Despite the awkward weight around her middle, she enjoyed strolling the short distance and inhaling the sea breeze from the small-boat harbor for which the town of Safe Harbor was named. It lay only about a mile away, visible from the upper stories of the medical center.

Her thoughts returned to the news that she carried a little girl. How exciting! Not that a boy wouldn't be wonderful, too. Still, Kate had never had a daughter.

Even if she's only mine until she's born.

As she entered the lobby, she saw a scant handful of people occupying the comfortable couches or browsing through the glass-front gift shop. It was a far cry from a few weeks earlier, when the news media had packed the place.

They'd been covering an influx of young mothers surrendering babies under the state's Safe Haven law, which was designed to encourage women not to abandon infants under unsafe conditions. Most had come after an Internet reporter named Ian Martin confused the name Safe Harbor with Safe Haven, implying that the medical facility offered special services.

As staff attorney, Tony had appeared on TV, explaining how the law protected the mothers from prosecution. *Naturally, he's been busy,* Kate thought. *I'm not the only thing he and Esther have to worry about.*

As she rode the elevator, she recalled the first time she'd met the couple, in a conference room here at the hospital. Esther had been tall and striking, thin as a model, with sleek sunlit hair and a tailored linen suit. But it was Tony who'd strode forward to clasp Kate's hand, his green eyes welcoming. He would make a wonderful father, she'd known instinctively.

Now, as Kate stepped onto the fifth floor, Dr. Rayburn's question echoed in her mind—*Have you talked to either of the Francos this week?*—along with something else he'd said: *In this kind of situation, communication is essential.*

Had he been referring only to the gender issue? Kate wiped her palms against her maternity jeans and approached the administrative suite.

The secretary, whose nameplate read May Chong, greeted Kate. "Mrs. Evans? Go on in. Mr. Franco's expecting you."

Kate tapped on the inner door before opening it. She'd come to this office once before, to sign the contract; not much had changed, she saw as she ventured inside. Same expanse of carpet, same large window providing a glimpse of the Pacific, same crammed bookshelves and broad desk.

But the man behind it looked different from the last time she'd seen him, about a month earlier. As Tony got to his feet, a frown darkened his usually amiable features, and the thick rust-brown hair not only needed a trim but flopped every which way, as if he'd been finger-combing it all morning.

When they shook hands, an awareness of him quivered through Kate. His strength. His kindness. And, today, his confusion.

"What's wrong?" she blurted. "Did Dr. Rayburn tell you about the baby?"

He regarded her quizzically. "What about the baby?"

"It's a girl." Seeing no reaction, Kate added, "Instead of a boy."

"A girl," he repeated, as if struggling to absorb the information.

"What gives, Tony?" she asked. "Where's Esther? Why is everyone acting so strange?"

In the fraction of a second before he answered, she could tell she hadn't imagined any of this. Something *had* happened.

"She's left me," he said in a stunned voice. "Picked up and moved across the country to start a new life."

As Kate sank into a chair, the baby wriggled. For once, she didn't respond. "How can she do that?"

"Don't worry—nothing's changed," Tony added quickly. "Not where you're concerned."

He was wrong about that, Kate noted dazedly. Everything had changed.

Chapter Two

The last person in the world Tony wanted to drag into this mess was the woman sitting across from him. From the moment they met, he'd liked Kate's sweet, honest face and golden brown eyes. He'd even hoped—foolishly, he saw now—that her mothering instincts might rub off on Esther.

A phrase popped into his mind: the willing suspension of disbelief. That described the way moviegoers allowed themselves to accept for the span of a few hours that Ms. or Mr. Famous-Movie-Star was really an impoverished waif or a Roman gladiator.

It wasn't supposed to apply to lawyers in their real lives. Yet he found himself guilty as charged.

Ever since he and Esther met in law school, he'd known her to be determined and driven, qualities that he'd admired. He hadn't considered her anything more than a fellow attorney, however, until they met again five years ago at an alumni event and connected at a deeper level. Or so he'd believed.

These days, he wasn't sure Esther had a deeper level.

"She left you?" Kate repeated in a small voice. "You mean she's having an affair?"

"No. She didn't leave me for another man." Tony felt certain on that account. Esther's goal was to be Ms. Powerful, not Mrs. Somebody-Else. "Without telling me, she's been angling for a high-powered job with the U.S. Attorney General's office. Now that she's landed it, she's moving to Washington."

"You won't go with her?" Ah, those wide, naive eyes. No, not naive; trusting. Tony was the one who'd acted naively, believing he and Esther were building a future together here in Orange County and that she could be happy balancing the roles of wife, mother and prosecutor.

He had trouble admitting this next part, but Kate had a right to know. "I said I'd consider relocating, but she prefers being unaccountable to anyone, including me."

"Well, she's a lamebrain!"

Her response made him laugh for the first time in days. "Thanks for the support."

"You're her *husband!*" Kate went on, bristling in outrage.

Tony chose his words cautiously, because despite his anger, he was trying to avoid turning his divorce into a battle to the death. "My wife's ambitious. I suspect she sees herself as a future Attorney General or Supreme Court justice. I respect her for that, but on a personal level, she's a very selfish woman." What else was there to say?

He'd been troubled when she'd announced the move a few weeks ago, but had assumed they could figure out a way to maintain their marriage, especially with a child on the way. Then, last night on the phone, she'd made it clear that staying married to a low-key staff attorney and having a baby in the house didn't fit her new image as a power player.

"Maybe she's just afraid you really don't want to give up your job." Kate flexed her hands. "I bet she's waiting for you to show that you're behind her one hundred percent by resigning."

"That's what I thought initially." He couldn't keep the edge from his voice. "Yesterday she demanded I agree to a dissolution of marriage as quickly as possible. She insists on her freedom, and the sooner the better."

Without realizing it, he'd leaned forward until their faces were inches apart. Abruptly Tony felt keenly attuned to Kate's velvety skin, her full mouth, her lushness. And to the tender, aching way she gazed at him, as if unable to believe any woman would leave him.

Esther's rejection hurt, in all sorts of ways. Kate's appreciation stirred him at the most basic level.

He must be out of his mind. Drawing back, Tony finger-combed his hair as he'd been doing all morning. Kate was the mother of his child. He had an obligation to protect her, not take advantage of her, even assuming she'd be willing, which he most certainly did *not* believe.

Also, he was still a married man, for however many months it took the divorce to go through. He'd agreed to it, naturally. Why would anyone try to hold on to a woman who didn't love him?

Kate folded her hands on her bulge. It was such an instinctive, unstudied act that Tony felt an urge to hug her. Right now, he craved instinctive, unstudied acts instead of calculating, self-serving…

He had to stop ranting about Esther, even if it was only in his brain.

"She can't expect to raise a baby alone while holding down a job like that," Kate said worriedly. "How many hours a week does she work? Sixty or seventy?"

"Make that eighty or ninety." Ah, yes. The whole subject of Esther's maternal instincts, or lack thereof, had been certain to surface.

"Then what's she going to do about your daughter?"

"She prefers that I keep the baby." Her actual words

had been far less diplomatic. *It's your DNA, buster. You raise it.*

Lovely sentiment. He'd like to see that comment engraved on a plaque and hung on the wall next to Esther's diplomas.

Kate hugged herself in apparent disbelief. "She was so excited. Remember how she kept saying what a wonderful thing I was doing?"

"Esther can be charming when she wants something," Tony conceded. "At her high-energy, charismatic best, she's hard to resist." He'd found her the kind of dazzling woman a man was proud to be seen with.

His more restrained nature had seemed to dovetail with hers. He'd gotten a thrill from accompanying his wife to political and social events and watching her work the crowd. He hadn't minded sharing or even ceding the limelight.

"Charming, charismatic and fickle?" Kate filled in.

"Exactly." He might as well be ruthlessly honest. "These past two years, she's been restless. Turning thirty seemed to rev up her biological clock, and when she discovered she had ovarian failure, that threw her into overdrive. Esther can't bear to fail at anything."

"But she wanted a baby. Surely she still does. Kids are precious," Kate added wistfully.

Tony's heart squeezed. They'd been terribly unfair to this generous woman. The substantial amount they were paying could never compensate for what she was giving up. "Yes, they are."

Her eyes met his with sudden intensity. "What about you? Are you prepared to raise a child on your own, or was this just Esther's idea?"

A fair question. Luckily, he didn't have to search for an answer. "The idea may have come from her, but once we met you and saw pictures of your little boy, having a child became the most important thing I'd ever wanted to do. When we learned you were pregnant, I stayed awake all night, too keyed up to sleep."

Her eyes sparkled. "Really?"

He'd purposely refrained from showing the true depth of his excitement to avoid making Esther feel that somehow the baby was more his than hers. But obviously, it hadn't worked.

"After my wife got bored with shopping for baby gear, I had fun ordering supplies on the Internet. Bought a few parenting books, too, although I'm still getting around to reading them." He'd also hired a decorator for the nursery. And he'd cherished daydreams of playing with his son.

Wait a minute. "It's a girl, you said?" Tony waved away his comment. "Of course you did. Well, the bond between fathers and daughters is extra-special."

"My dad was our anchor," Kate murmured. "For me, my mom and my sister. I'm so glad he was alive to walk me down the aisle at my wedding."

"He's gone, then? I'm sorry."

"Lung cancer," she replied. "Before Brady was born. I wish he'd never smoked." She shifted in her seat as if to shake off the memories. "The childbirth class starts tomorrow night at seven. It's downstairs here at the hospital. Esther was supposed to go with me, but obviously that's out."

Was she inviting *him* to attend? Well, the more he learned about babies, the better. "I'll be there."

"You're sure? I could ask my mother."

"No way I'm missing my daughter's entrance into the world. This does mean I get to be present, doesn't it?" he asked eagerly.

When she smiled, the room glowed. "Absolutely."

"Great." He couldn't ignore the message light blinking on his phone any longer. "I'm glad you stopped by."

"So am I." Kate started to rise, but didn't get far. The chair must have been deeper than she expected, because she teetered off balance.

Leaping to his feet, Tony caught her arm. "Let me help."

"Thanks." She swayed against him, her heady scent flooding his senses like a bouquet of flowers.

"You smell nice," Tony blurted. Wait! He had no business implying anything personal. "I mean, that's lovely perfume. Like a spring garden."

"It's my shampoo." Kate's bulge brushed him as she straightened.

Tony could have sworn something kicked him in the hip. "Was that my daughter?"

Kate beamed. "She's feisty."

"With a kick like that, she should go out for soccer."

"I think it was an elbow. Practicing her karate moves." She ran a hand lightly up his biceps. "Better get in shape so you can keep up with her, Dad. Not that you aren't already." When she plucked her hand away, he could have sworn she was blushing. "Sorry. How silly of me."

He'd enjoyed that casual contact more than he ought to. "Tomorrow night," he confirmed, and retreated to a safe distance.

"Wear comfortable clothes," Kate advised and strolled off, leaving behind that faint but tantalizing scent.

Tony returned to reviewing a contract with one of the hospital's vendors, but his mind refused to cooperate. As he reached for the phone to pick up his messages. he wondered exactly what constituted a safe distance and how he was going to maintain it during a childbirth class.

Or whether he truly wanted to.

NEARLY ONE O'CLOCK. Kate was running late and her stomach had begun rumbling. Then the ignition on her car, an aging sedan that had relied on her late husband Quinn's expertise as a mechanic to keep it running, took three tries before it sparked.

She made the ten-minute drive straight to her sister's house. Mary Beth had promised to pick up Brady at kindergarten along with two five-year-olds who attended her home day-care center.

The ranch-style home lay in a cul-de-sac near Safe Harbor's northern edge. A stand of trees blocked the sight of the freeway a quarter of a mile off, but as Kate hefted herself from the car, she noted the ever-present hum of traffic.

She mounted the porch between a scraggly camellia bush and an overgrown azalea. Mary Beth used to be a stickler about gardening, but no wonder she'd fallen behind, with a pair of school-age sons, a home business and a husband who worked as an air traffic controller.

Kate tapped lightly, then let herself inside with her key. The house was quiet. No childish chatter or bodies hurtling about, which meant the children must be napping. She really *was* late.

Bypassing the formal living room, she picked a path between toys and books in the den and found her sister and mother in the kitchen, sipping coffee at the well-worn table. Irene Mulligan's face, more wrinkled than before her heart attack a year ago, filled with delight when she caught sight of her younger daughter.

"Everything okay at the doctor's?" Mary Beth tucked a wayward strand of ash-blond hair behind her ear. The dark roots needed a touch-up, Kate noted with professional interest, but her sister always declined her offers.

"Well, sort of." Before rushing into the latest developments, she added, "I'm sorry you had to fix lunch for Brady. I meant to be here sooner."

"I made his sandwich," Irene volunteered.

"Mom tucked him in for his nap, too." After their mother's heart attack, Mary Beth had insisted that Irene move into the four-bedroom home, and their mom really did enjoy being around all the activity. Now that she'd stabilized on medication, Irene had an excellent prognosis, but neither of her daughters could bear to think of her living alone again.

"Thanks, Mom." Kate fixed herself a sandwich from the peanut butter, jelly and bread on the counter. "Here's my first big news. Turns out Arthur is a girl."

"A girl named Arthur?" Her mother smiled.

"Finally a girl in the family!" Mary Beth exclaimed. "Not that I'll ever get to hold her."

Her sister's disapproval of the surrogacy made it doubly hard to drop the next revelation, but there was no avoiding it. "I had a meeting with Tony." She plunged ahead. "He and Esther are getting a divorce."

"Oh, dear," Irene said.

"Well, that's just great." Mary Beth smacked her hand on the table, rattling the cups, then glanced worriedly toward the interior of the house. No sounds arose from her half-dozen charges, however. "On top of everything else, the baby gets born into a broken home."

As she poured herself a glass of milk, Kate explained the situation, finishing with, "Tony's going to be a wonderful dad."

"Yes, but what about a mother?" Irene said.

"You should keep the baby," Mary Beth insisted. "This isn't the deal you signed up for, and she's *your* daughter. I told you, according to a friend of Ray's, you have legal grounds to fight this."

Wolfing her sandwich, Kate shook her head rather than argue. Not only had she signed a contract, she'd made a promise to the Francos...to Tony. Besides, Kate had Brady's future and her own to think about. How could she work and study nursing, the way she'd planned, if she had a baby to care for?

All the same, her hand strayed to her bulge. No movement, which meant Ariel—her new name for the baby—must be napping like the other kids. Kate pictured the little girl curled in Brady's old crib, fist jammed in her mouth, a soft pink onesie stretching to her tiny feet.

Perhaps she could suggest Tony put the baby in day care with Mary Beth. On second thought, probably not a good idea. Her sister was too possessive about the baby already.

As the silence lengthened, Irene answered for her. "Kate has her own dreams to fulfill. She's worked hard all these years."

"And I haven't?" Mary Beth snapped.

Kate swallowed another mouthful of her sandwich. "Where did that come from?"

Irene patted her elder daughter's hand. "You work hard, also. Too hard."

The tension eased from Mary Beth's shoulders. "I'm sorry, guys. The kids were cranky this morning and Ray's been putting in extra shifts. I didn't mean to take it out on you."

Kate studied her sister sympathetically. Four years older, Mary Beth had excelled in school and earned a bachelor's degree and teaching credential, unlike Kate, who'd barely squeaked through two years at community college. Energetic and confident, Mary Beth had never seemed to flag. Until today.

"Are you sure you're okay?" Kate asked. "I didn't mean to stick you with Brady for so long."

"He's fine. In fact, he's adorable." Mary Beth looked embarrassed by her outburst. "As for dreams, I'm living mine. It may not be quite how I'd pictured it, but I feel very lucky. And I think it's wonderful that you're going to be a nurse."

"Thanks. I don't know what I'd do without you," Kate admitted.

She, too, felt lucky, despite the loss of her husband and the challenges that lay ahead. So what if she'd struggled financially these past few years? It was worth every day of standing on her feet and every night of juggling bills when she had such a loving family.

A short while later, she strapped a freshly awakened Brady into the car. Kate's heart felt full as she kissed the little boy's soft cheek and felt his arms twine around her.

Like her, Tony would surely rise to the demands of single parenthood. Maybe he hadn't quite grasped what lay ahead yet, but she intended to help him.

They'd all make it through just fine.

Chapter Three

Tony spent most of Wednesday afternoon preparing for and conducting a workshop about a topic most physicians preferred to avoid: lawsuits. Specifically, how to prevent them.

"Legal experts used to believe the best way to deal with situations where patients suffered harm was to limit or completely cut off communication with their families," he told a dozen specialists who'd gathered in the small fourth-floor auditorium.

"Why would anyone do that?" Despite being one of the youngest members on staff, neonatologist Jared Sellers never shied away from speaking his mind. "It's cruel."

"The latest findings agree with you," Tony said. "Whether or not the physician was at fault, people look for someone to blame. They're hurt, they're suffering and they're angry. We now know that simply saying 'I'm terribly sorry' can defuse some of that anger."

"But doesn't that imply that we're guilty of something?" asked a surgeon. "I can't save every patient. It's unrealistic for families to expect that."

"Good point." Tony didn't bother to check his notes; the words simply flowed. "It's one thing to provide medical information about what happened and express regret. It's something else to become overly emotional and make statements such as 'This shouldn't have happened' that can be used against you in court."

"But I feel that way when I lose a baby, even if I've done everything I can," Jared protested.

"It's natural to second-guess your decisions," Tony agreed. "But you don't have to do that in front of the patient's family. Let's talk about how we can communicate honestly without incriminating ourselves."

He continued, mixing information gleaned from a recent legal conference with observations from reading and from his own experience. Tony enjoyed this part of his job far more than paper-shuffling. He didn't mind that he'd have to repeat the same information at future meetings, since not all staff and consulting doctors could be present at the same time.

Questions kept him longer than he'd intended. He'd had to schedule the gathering for 5:30 p.m. to accommodate the doctors, and it was a few minutes past seven by the time the group broke up.

Tony had grabbed a power bar around 4:00 p.m. That would have to hold him for now.

Childbirth classes were held—ironically, in Tony's view—in the workout room on the ground floor. He arrived as a stocky woman with silver-touched dark hair was closing the door.

"Ah," she said. "You must be our missing partner."

Never mind that he'd been lecturing the doctor-gods of the hospital, he'd just been reduced to the status of lowly truant.

Scooting inside, Tony found all eyes fixed on him. He counted seven couples—well, six couples plus Kate—sitting on mats.

They had to be kidding. Hugely pregnant women on the floor? Not to mention the dads and a few female partners, all sensibly clad in sweat suits, jeans or shorts. Ruefully loosening his tie, Tony conceded that he'd forgotten Kate's advice about wearing comfortable clothes.

Awkwardly, he folded himself onto the mat beside her. Darned if her face wasn't bright with amusement.

"What?" he asked in a low voice.

"You made it."

"Well, sure."

"I like your idea of casual dress." She indicated his dark-blue suit, pinstriped shirt and silk tie. "Do you starch and iron your pj's, too?"

Tony smiled. "Only for pajama parties."

She grinned back at him. What a delight. If Esther had been sitting here ballooned out and forced to wait alone in a roomful of couples, he'd have been lucky to escape with superficial lacerations.

A voice from the front called them to attention. "Hi, I'm Tina Torres," announced the stocky woman. "I'm a certified childbirth instructor and I have three children of my own, so I understand what you're going through. Tonight, we're going to talk about a range of issues from pain to exercise to nutrition."

Guiltily, Tony remembered the power bar. But she didn't mean nutrition for the *dads*.

He peered at Kate to see how she was reacting to all this, and caught the sparkle of a tear on her cheek. Perhaps she was remembering her previous classes with her husband.

Since other partners had slid an arm around the women they were with to offer support, he did the same. When Kate shot him a startled glance, he nearly withdrew, but then she leaned a little closer. He enjoyed the light pressure on his shoulder, and the sense that he was offering her protection.

The instructor was discussing pain, he discovered when

he tuned back in. Tony had expected her to soft-pedal the subject with words such as *discomfort* and *pressure*. Not Ms. Torres.

"Lots of things cause pain during labor. For instance, that's an awfully big baby to come out through an awfully small place." She pointed to a diagram on the wall.

Tony didn't like associating that clinical illustration with the soft woman at his side, because thinking about the challenge she faced brought home the fact that he'd put her in this condition. Of her own free will, but nevertheless, men were supposed to take care of women, not subject them to physical near impossibilities.

"Another cause of pain is repeated muscle contractions. Partners, I want you to try something. Those of you who've already given birth can skip this part," Tina added. "Now, make a fist."

Tony complied. Easy enough.

"Open and close it. Keep doing that. I'll tell you when to stop." The instructor regarded her watch.

After a few seconds, he noticed a tight feeling in his hand. Then the muscle started to burn. Since he had a good golf grip, Tony considered his hands fairly strong, but it wasn't long before pain snaked up his arm.

"Stop," Tina said. Tony shook out his hand. "That was sixty seconds. Imagine doing that for hours with your whole abdomen."

He'd rather not.

"Moms, if you're tense or frightened, it will increase your pain. In these classes, we're going to work on ways to break the cycle of fear and pain…"

His cell phone rang, echoing in Tony's ears like a fire alarm. Embarrassed, he flipped it open.

Esther.

"I'll just be a minute," he murmured to Kate. She gave a hesitant nod, and Tony hurried from the room.

He supposed he should ignore the call, but given Esther's work as a prosecutor, he'd always worried about her. Over the years, she'd racked up quite a few hardened criminals as enemies, and long hours meant that she often walked out to her car alone at night.

It was after 10:00 p.m. in D.C. Although she hadn't had time to score any enemies there, surely she wouldn't call unless it was urgent.

"Hey," he answered. "What's up?"

"I've been thinking." Her calm tone of voice dispelled any concerns. "I want this whole divorce business over as fast as possible, so you should put the house on the market. Price it right and we might get a quick sale."

He couldn't believe her nerve. "Sell our house? I love that place."

"Well, it's half mine, and I want my money."

Yes, she was entitled to half. But not instantly. "Before or after the Christmas wedding reception you promised to host for your best friend?" Tony retorted sarcastically. "Oh, wait. You already bailed out on her. Matron of honor, weren't you?"

He hadn't meant to speak so loudly, or with such sarcasm. Tony surveyed the area to see if anyone had overheard. Nobody lingered in the hallway, but he did catch tantalizing scents from the nearby cafeteria, a reminder of his missed meal.

"There's no reason to get nasty," Esther snapped.

He refused to abandon the home where he wanted their daughter to grow up. "I'll have the house appraised and get a loan to buy out your half. That's standard in a divorce."

"Well, do it fast. I need a down payment for a condo of my own," she whined. "I hate rentals."

"Ain't my problem."

"Elegantly phrased, counselor," she sniped.

"Bite me. How do you like *that* phrasing?" About to turn off the phone, he realized he hadn't broken today's news. "By the way, we're having a girl. Not a boy."

"A girl?"

"Does that make a difference?" He didn't see why it would, and, frankly, wasn't sure he wanted it to. Yet despite his anger at his wife's behavior, Tony conceded that he'd be willing to try again. He and Esther had made commitments to each other and to this child. That mattered more than his hurt feelings, and it ought to matter more than her ambitions.

"Not really," she said. "I'll be flying out soon to file divorce papers. Get moving on that loan."

"Anything for my *wife*." Immediately regretting his angry retort, he turned off the phone. While Tony was determined not to become a boor, Esther could try the patience of a saint. The smell of hamburgers grilling and the answering growl of his stomach did nothing to soften his temper, either.

In this mood, he didn't see how he could go back into class. But he had to get a grip, for Kate's sake and his daughter's.

KATE'S CHEEKS burned with embarrassment. Despite the closed door, surely everyone in the room could hear snatches of the one-sided conversation in the hall, a continuing undercurrent to Tina's teaching. She doubted anyone missed the fact that Tony was arguing with his wife. They probably assumed she and her pregnancy had broken up a marriage.

She was so upset, she missed most of Tina's advice. By the time silence finally fell in the hall, the class was on hands and knees in the middle of an exercise called pelvic tilts. Luckily, Kate vaguely recalled how to do them from the last time around.

"Kind of reminds me of how I got pregnant in the first place, but that was more fun," one lady said, to a chorus of laughter.

I didn't even get the fun part. Kate blushed harder. Thank goodness she hadn't spoken aloud.

She wished Tony would hurry. In all fairness, though, Quinn had missed one of *their* classes to go on a motorcycle trip with buddies.

"On your feet, folks. This next exercise is best done with a partner." As Tina's voice rang out, Tony reentered.

He nodded apologetically to the instructor and approached Kate with a sheepish expression that soothed her annoyance. When he held out his hands, she took them gladly and followed the instructions to hold on to her partner and sink into a squat with her heels flat on the floor.

"Practice this every day for several minutes," the teacher said as Kate lurched to an upright position. "You can use a chair if your partner isn't around."

"Glad to know I can be replaced so easily," Tony murmured close to her ear, the rumble of his voice sending a tickle through her.

Kate wished she weren't so keenly aware of the strength of his hands in hers as she repeated the squat. And darned if this exercise didn't give her an awfully personal look at the length of him, all the way down past his appealingly skewed tie and etched leather belt to…never mind.

As she rose with considerable assistance, she registered his wonderful end-of-day scent, masculinity triumphing over the civilizing effect of morning showers and aftershave lotions. She missed being around a man when his natural scent broke through that veneer.

"How're you doing?" Tony held on to her even after she reached an upright position.

"Me? Fine."

Everyone else was settling onto the mats again, which left her and Tony standing there like a pair of starstruck lovers, holding hands in plain view. "We really have to stop meeting this way," he said, and received a smattering of applause as they sat down like the others.

Kate was grateful to see a fire extinguisher on the wall. If her cheeks grew any hotter, she might need it.

AFTER A DISCUSSION of proper diet and vitamins, the class ended with a few breathing exercises. Tony might have found them calming if the in-and-out movement of Kate's chest hadn't kept drawing his gaze. For heaven's sake, he was too mature and too sophisticated to stare at a pair of breasts, however beautifully formed.

Breathe in from the abdomen. Breathe out from the abdomen. Don't think about...

"We could hear you, you know," she muttered.

"What?" Around them, Tony realized, the class was breaking up. On their mat, Kate sat tugging at the V-neck of her short-sleeved jersey top. He hoped that didn't mean she'd noticed him staring.

"In the hall. Arguing."

What had he said, anyway? "Esther ordered me to hold a fire sale on our house. I guess my response wasn't very gentlemanly." When Kate stirred, he rose and once again assisted her to her feet.

Nearby, two women shouldering oversize purses peered at him and exchanged knowing glances.

"They probably think I broke up your marriage," Kate said.

"What?"

"You were obviously squabbling with your estranged wife." She brushed a speck of lint from her maternity top. "I wish you'd turned off your phone before class started."

So did he, under the circumstances. Still, you never knew when an urgent call might come through. "I have to be available to the hospital 24/7."

She clasped her hands. "Have you considered how you're going to manage being a single parent? You can't raise a child only when you have nothing better to do. You have to be *present* for her."

He was in no mood for a scolding. "I plan to hire a full-time housekeeper as well as a nanny. There's also a child care center here at the hospital. My daughter will be well cared for."

"You mean she'll eat three meals a day and she won't fall in the swimming pool?" Kate shot back. "That isn't a family, that's a well-run orphanage. But then, abandoning one's baby, physically *or* emotionally, seems to be a popular pastime in Safe Harbor these days."

No sooner were the words out than she clapped a hand over her mouth. Stunned by her own outburst, evidently.

Tony felt stunned, too. His sweet little surrogate had a temper.

No matter what she believed, the fact was, he wanted his daughter fiercely. Raising her would be the most important thing he ever did in his life, even if he still couldn't imagine exactly what being a father entailed.

"We need to talk," he said.

"I… Tony, I'm sorry." Her hand rested lightly on his arm.

"I'm not angry," he clarified, touched by the alarm in her eyes. "What I am is hungry. Starving, which makes me cranky as a bear. Nevertheless, it's time we discussed our daughter's future and how I'm going to manage this alone. Care to join me for a bite?"

She withdrew her hand. "I have to pick up Brady at my sister's. I've taken far too much advantage of her already."

"This probably isn't a conversation we should have in the hospital cafeteria, anyway," Tony conceded. "Why don't we meet at your place later? I can help you put Brady to bed, if that's all right. I've never tucked a kid in. Guess I'd better start learning how."

She seemed to struggle for words. "I've never... Nobody's ever... I mean, that was his father's job."

"I've overstepped."

"Not exactly."

The room had emptied. Tony noticed Ms. Torres hovering by the light switch. "I'll get it," he called. "I'm the hospital's staff attorney. I'll take responsibility." With a nod, she departed.

"Actually, it *is* a good idea for us to talk." Kate lifted her chin. Since she was six or seven inches shorter than him, the gesture merely emphasized how cute and determined she was.

Determined. Understandable, since this was not only his baby but also hers for the next couple of months, Tony reflected. And for all his education, she was the one who possessed a vast knowledge of parenting.

Still, he hoped she wouldn't try to go back on their surrogacy agreement. Much as he appreciated her situation, he couldn't allow that.

"I'll try not to intrude on your privacy," he said. "But with the change in my circumstances, there are a few things we need to square away."

That came out sterner than he'd intended, and she jerked back. "All right."

"If you'd prefer to wait until another time…"

She shook her head. "Tonight will be fine. Give me an hour, okay?"

"Sure." He knew her address, since he and Esther had visited the cozy home a few miles inland when they first contracted with Kate. It had seemed a wise precaution to make sure their surrogate lived under healthy circumstances.

He'd liked the cheerful interior and the smell of baking. She'd offered brownies, which he'd gladly accepted and Esther had declined. His soon-to-be ex survived mostly on salads and diet drinks.

Following Kate out of the room, Tony switched off the lights. "Let me walk you to your car."

She waved away the offer. "I'm fine. Go eat."

He supposed he'd better. He needed sustenance for the evening ahead.

In the lobby, as Kate walked away, Tony noticed how the swell of her figure begged for the curve of his hand. He'd never imagined pregnancy could make a woman so alluring.

What was wrong with him? Getting a divorce was no excuse for indulging crazy impulses. Determined to regain control of his thoughts, Tony headed for the cafeteria to satisfy a different kind of hunger.

Chapter Four

"Joey brought his daddy to school for show-and-tell, 'cause he's got a cool job." Brady perched on the edge of the bed, swinging his feet. When he lay still, the twin-size bed swallowed up his five-year-old frame, but he hardly ever lay still unless sound asleep.

"What does his father do?" Sitting beside him, Kate struggled not to check her watch. Although she'd told her son that the baby's father—she'd long ago explained the surrogacy to Brady—would be stopping by, she'd assured him they had plenty of time for their night-night ritual. By her latest calculations, they had fifteen minutes to go.

The ritual had changed since Quinn's death. He used to read their son stories, but after he died, Brady had refused to accept Kate as a substitute reader. Instead, she read to him earlier in the day, and had launched a new bedtime tradition of recapping the day's events. As a result, she'd learned a great deal about the routine at kindergarten, including show-and-tell.

"He's a fireman," he said. "What does the baby's daddy do?"

"He's a lawyer." How did you describe *that* to kid? "He helps people understand grown-up rules."

"Like don't speed on the freeway?"

"That's a policeman's job." Kate tried to figure out a

simple example. "More like…when you sign your name to a promise, you have to keep it."

He looked puzzled. "We always have to keep promises."

"We try our best," she agreed. "But when it's a contract in writing, we can be forced to keep our word, even if…" Darn, this was complicated! "…even if things have changed."

His attention shifted to her tummy. "Why is the baby a girl?"

Since she'd broken the news to Brady, he'd asked the same question over and over, apparently struggling to wrap his mind around the change. Kate gave the same answer now that she had before. "The baby was always a girl. The doctor didn't figure it out until now."

"I want a brother."

"That doesn't change her gender," she said patiently. "Anyway, I told you, the baby won't live here."

"But I *might* see him at the park."

"Might see *her*."

"Okay." Brady yawned and stretched. The fine blond hair tumbling on his forehead reminded her of Quinn's. So did those slate-gray eyes that occasionally seemed wise beyond his years and at other times brimmed with mischief.

"Tomorrow I'm giving you a haircut." She kept a pair of clippers handy for that task. "All right?"

"Sure, Mommy." Sleepily, he slid beneath the covers and pulled them up to his chin. Tucking him in was another task he'd refused to hand over to her after Quinn's death.

Kate dimmed the lights, leaving the door open a crack. The boy's bedroom lay directly across from hers, with the bathroom close by. Not much extra space in this house, but she liked its coziness.

In the kitchen, she arranged a plate of oatmeal-raisin cookies, which she considered nutritious enough to meet Tina Torres's requirements.

She'd enjoyed the class tonight. Kate missed being around people since taking leave from her job a few weeks earlier. And it had been fun exercising with Tony. He had the most delightful, teasing grin. But what had he meant by "a few things we need to square away"?

Restlessly, she smoothed the slipcovers on the living room couch and chairs, and ran a hand over the large chest that did double duty as a coffee table and storage unit. At an end table covered with framed photos, Kate paused.

As always, the sight of Quinn took her breath away. Head thrown back, hair blowing, he laughed at the camera from astride his motorcycle. What a daredevil he'd been, and what a love affair he'd had with anything motorized. The day he took a busted all-terrain vehicle as payment for repairing a boat engine had been a highlight for him.

When he got the ATV up and running, Kate had stood firm against letting Brady ride on it. Quinn had reluctantly agreed that, at age three, their son was too young to be a passenger.

One weekend when her husband felt the urge to blow off steam, he and a friend had trucked it a few hours inland to the desert for a day of tooling around. In what was planned as the last ride of the day, Quinn had zoomed over a sand dune without realizing another fun-loving guy was doing the same from the opposite direction.

The other man had escaped with a broken collarbone. When the ATV overturned, Quinn hit his head on a rock and died a few hours later. A freak accident, the police had called it. Kate had barely made it to the hospital in time to say goodbye.

Her eyes burned as she studied her late husband's

carefree image. *Oh, Quinn, you were supposed to be here to watch Brady grow up.*

She swallowed the lump in her throat. Until this pregnancy, she'd broken down weeping almost daily, unable even to think about the future. Now, although the sadness lingered, she felt the past receding more and more.

Her gaze skimmed to the newest addition to her picture gallery. Tony and Esther resembled fashion models in their stylish suits, Tony turned toward his wife and Esther facing the camera.

Kate felt a sudden wave of dislike. Esther hadn't only abandoned her husband, she'd also gone back on a commitment to Kate and the baby. This woman didn't deserve a place of honor.

But Tony did. Was there some way to delete Esther without damaging the picture?

A toy catalog lay on the floor, where Brady had been cutting out pictures with blunt-tipped scissors. Impulsively, Kate picked up the instrument, clipped a shot of a teddy bear, and taped it over the frame so it blocked Esther's image.

Much better.

The doorbell rang, startling her. She'd meant to listen for Tony's car on their quiet street. Then she remembered that he drove a super-quiet luxury car. No wonder she hadn't heard it.

Kate peered into a framed mirror in the dining alcove, and immediately wished she hadn't. Nothing to be done about her faded makeup, so she gathered her courage and went to admit her guest.

He looked more relaxed, now that he'd eaten. And he must have stopped by his house, because he'd changed into jeans and a polo shirt.

"Hi." As a precaution, Kate added, "Brady's in bed."

"I'll keep my voice down." He held out a children's book. "It's for Brady."

Kate read the title. *"Ben and Me."*

"It was one of my favorites as a child."

Too advanced for a five-year-old, she noted as she leafed through it, but Brady would enjoy it soon enough. "That's very kind of you."

"Not at all." Strolling into the living room, Tony gravitated to the photo display. As he picked up the frame, Kate wondered in a rush of embarrassment why she hadn't waited until *after* his visit to alter the picture. "Well, well."

"That was childish of me," she apologized.

Tony grinned. "I'm not sure marriage to a teddy bear would be legal in the state of California, but it does look cuddly."

"I can remove it," she offered.

"Why? Esther's chosen to be figuratively out of the picture, so why not literally, as well?" He moved to the couch. "Please sit down, Kate. I made a few notes." From his pocket, he retrieved his smart phone.

Feeling like a kid called into the principal's office, she chose a chair on the far side of the room. Might as well get this over with.

"You look as if you're facing a firing squad," Tony said gently, and shifted to the end of the sofa closest to her. "I'm only trying to prevent misunderstandings."

"Making sure I understand the grown-up rules," she murmured.

"What?"

"Brady asked me what a lawyer does, and I said you make sure grown-ups know what the rules are."

"As usual, you go straight to the heart of the matter." He regarded her appreciatively.

Much as she enjoyed his attention, Kate itched to get on with this. "Well, what *are* the rules?"

He let out a long breath. "First, I'm the father of this baby, and until she signs divorce papers, Esther is the mother. Are we in agreement?"

Kate nodded. She hadn't indicated otherwise, had she?

Tony studied the small screen. "Second, I respect your expertise as a mother and I welcome your input." When she didn't respond, he added, "That means I'd appreciate any advice you can offer about becoming a dad. My parents are both dead and I don't have any close family to consult. Just a bachelor brother."

He had a whole hospital full of nurses and pediatricians who would no doubt ply him with suggestions, but that wasn't the same, Kate supposed. "I'd be glad to help."

He reached his third point. "Your assistance is purely voluntary. You don't owe me anything."

"Got it."

"Finally, your role with the baby ends with its birth."

"Her birth," Kate corrected.

"What did I say?"

"Its birth." She didn't mean to be argumentative. "I understand that I'm the surrogate. As long as you provide a good home, I'll hold up my end of the bargain." No matter how many doubts she entertained, ultimately she needed to live with the pact they'd made.

He stuck the device in his pocket. "I didn't mean to sound pompous."

Best to avoid discussing *that* subject after he'd just laid a bureaucratic load on her. "Have you thought about a name?" she asked, instead.

"No, I... We can't go with Arthur anymore, can we?" he teased. "Artemis? Ariadne? I'm joking, by the way."

"What was your mother's name?" That seemed the sensible place to start.

"Cornelia," he said. "I'm not sticking this kid with the nickname Cornie."

"Grandmothers?"

"Old-fashioned names, both of them. Esther's family doesn't count, for obvious reasons."

"Any other female relatives?" she persisted.

He thrust a hand through his hair, making it haywire once more. "I should have thought of that sooner. I had a little sister who died when she was eleven. Tara."

"That's a lovely name." It fit with Kate's part-Irish heritage, too. Best not to bring that up, though. "Do you mind if I ask what happened to her?"

He stared pensively into the distance. "She was born with spina bifida. That's a condition affecting the neural tube, the nerves that run along your spine. She walked with crutches and caught lung infections easily, but she was perfectly normal in most ways."

"What causes the condition?" Kate had never known anyone with it, although it was one of the conditions her prenatal blood test had screened for. With negative results, fortunately.

"Genetics, or a deficiency of folic acid—vitamin B9—in the mother. That's one of the reasons Dr. Rayburn prescribed vitamins before you got pregnant, as you'll recall. In Tara's case, we never knew the cause. I used to wish I could give her some of my good health."

"You must have loved her a lot."

His mouth quirked. "Oh, she drove me crazy. Like any kid, she could be cranky and demanding, but also a real sweetheart. Being six years older, I felt protective. I should have been a lot more protective, damn it."

His vehemence surprised Kate. "Why?"

"Just…never mind. Too late to change anything now."

"What did she die of?" Kate hoped this wasn't too sensitive a topic.

"Pneumonia," he said tautly. "The antibiotic-resistant kind. Mom never recovered from losing her. None of us did."

"Is that what attracted you to working in a hospital? Because you understand what it's like for patients and their families?"

His eyebrows knitted into a firm line. "Now there's an idea I hadn't considered. I worked in family law initially, but there was an overlap with health issues that affect families. Things like durable powers of attorney for health care and living wills, malpractice law, how to handle end-of-life issues. I gravitated to that part of the practice more and more, and when this job opened up three years ago, I went for it."

Kate had run out of questions. Getting back to their earlier topic, she said, "I'm glad you chose the name Tara. It just feels right."

"To me, too." His gaze met Kate's. "Oh! I forgot something."

Not another rule. "Oh?"

"I'd like to repay you for any time you're willing to give me, now that the situation's changed," Tony said. "Such as meeting with me this evening. And I could use advice setting up my house for a baby."

"You're already paying me plenty."

He handed her the card of a handyman service. "During the next couple of months, if you have any problems with plumbing, electricity or other home repairs, give them a call and have them send me the bill. I'd offer to fix things myself, but that would be more a menace than a favor."

She might as well accept. Certainly Kate could use the

help. "Thanks. I usually do my own repairs but I can't exactly crawl under the sink anymore." She wished she had a gift in return, since he'd brought the book, too. Then she remembered. "Cookies!"

From the way Tony's face lit up, she could tell she'd scored a hit. "Wonderful." He went with her to the kitchen, where he inhaled with obvious pleasure. "Smells like a real home. I'll have to learn to bake."

"It's easy." She set the plate on the table. "Dig in."

"Ladies first."

"You're the guest."

They both said "okay" and reached at the same moment. Their hands met in the middle of the plate.

Tony's cupped her palm and, as if by instinct, his fingers interlaced with hers. Kate's gaze fixed on the muscles in his wrist and arm. She felt enveloped and wonderfully sheltered. A moment later, with a trace of reluctance, he released his grip. "Guess we're both hungry."

In more ways than one. Oh, how she missed having a man to touch her and share her life. "They're good cookies," she mumbled distractedly, and took one.

Tony bit into his and let out a sigh. "Heavenly."

She let the sweet taste melt in her mouth. "Milk?" she asked when it faded.

"Sure."

Kate bustled about, trying not to think about that brief contact. They were both lonely. That's all it meant.

"Mommy?" said a little voice as she finished putting away the milk.

Uh-oh. A small, pajama-clad figure stood rubbing his eyes in front of the table. "You're supposed to be in bed."

"Cookie?" Brady asked.

Tony regarded the imp with fascination. "Is it okay to give him one?"

"He already brushed his teeth. Besides, he ate several earlier. Too much sugar isn't good for kids." She touched her son's shoulder. "Honey, Mr. Franco and I have grown-up stuff to discuss. You should go back to sleep."

He folded his arms. "My eyes are too wakey."

"They aren't going to close while you're standing in the middle of the kitchen," Kate pointed out.

Doggedly, Brady held his ground. "Somebody has to tuck me in."

"But you never let me…."

He was staring longingly at Tony. Kate's heart squeezed as she realized how much her son missed having a man in the house.

"That was his father's job," she explained. "He hasn't let me tuck him in since he was a toddler."

"Well, I *am* supposed to learn how to do these things. Is it okay if I pinch-hit?"

"Go ahead."

Tony took a swig of his milk and got up. "Lead on, sport."

Brady slipped his small hand into Tony's big one. *Those hands are the right size for both of us*, Kate thought.

But only for tonight.

In the bedroom, Brady climbed between the sheets. Tony sat down, then realized he couldn't tug the comforter into place while he was on it, so he stood to complete the task. He pulled so hard that, when he let go, the covers draped over Brady's mouth. "This is more complicated than it looks."

Kate chuckled at the sight of the take-charge attorney fumbling with bedcovers. "You'll get the hang of it."

The boy made a rude noise with his lips.

Tony folded the edge of the sheets back. "How's that?"

"Book," Brady demanded.

Tony look questioningly at Kate. "Is this part of the ritual, too?"

She averted her face so he wouldn't see the sudden sheen in her eyes. "The daddy part." From a low shelf, she chose a favorite and handed it to him.

"Where the Wild Things Are." Tony scanned a page. "I guess that book I brought is for older kids."

"He'll grow into it."

"Don't talk. Read!" Brady ordered.

"You're a bossy little guy," Tony said.

He looked contrite. "I'm sorry."

Tony brushed a thumb across the boy's temple. "That's okay. I get crabby when I wake up in the middle of the night, too."

Then he settled and began to read, his voice low and firm. Brady's face softened as he listened to the beloved tale.

The way Tony caressed the words, squeaking some and growling others, clearly gave him as much pleasure as it did her son. Kate could picture him sitting at Tara's bedside, night after night, delighting them both.

He *was* good at this.

After a while, Brady's lids drooped and his breathing eased. Tony stopped reading. He observed the sleeping child for a moment before rising and slipping out with Kate.

"He's adorable," he murmured.

"He misses his daddy," she said. "I had hoped my brother-in-law would fill some of the void, but he's got a high-pressure job and two kids of his own."

In the living room, Tony lingered near the door. "I don't

like the fact that Tara will grow up without a mom. I keep hoping Esther will rethink her decision. Once the initial excitement wears off, maybe she'll realize how much she's sacrificing."

"You'd take her back?" Kate ventured.

"A part of me still feels married," he said thoughtfully. "I admit, I'm angry, but it's not as if she's having an affair. I've always been proud of Esther's drive, her wins in court, her honors and awards. And I've let the relationship part of our marriage drift as much as she has. Except for choosing to have a baby, we haven't talked much in years about anything that matters."

"You honestly think she'll come back?" She ought to be pleased at the prospect. Instead, Kate felt torn. Could a woman who cast aside her commitments this way really become a good mother?

"If she'd been able to get pregnant, things might have been different. It's possible that, in a way, she's still reacting to the disappointment." Tony glanced toward the teddybear photo as if seeing the underlying image of Esther, movie-star beautiful and radiating assurance. "At some level, I keep feeling that our marriage isn't over."

"I hope you're right."

Egotistical people sometimes doted on their kids, Kate supposed. At the salon, she had clients like that, insensitive to almost everyone except their adored children.

"Well, I'd better go." Instead of moving, though, Tony let his gaze linger on the modest room. Kate became acutely aware of the old quilt tossed over the back of the sofa and a couple of toy trucks Brady had left on the carpet. "I like this place. Makes my house seem kind of cold."

Cold but magazine-quality gorgeous. "Hold on. You might be suffering from cookie interruptus, and we've got plenty. Let me wrap some for you."

He caught her elbow. "Save those for Brady. Besides, we're both supposed to watch what we eat, right?"

Standing so close, she could hardly breathe. Better not tilt her face toward his. No sense tempting fate. "Right." She eased back. "When do you suggest we start your daddy training? Or were you kidding about that?"

"I'm in deadly earnest." He consulted his phone calendar. "How does Saturday afternoon sound? We could look at the nursery and baby proofing, that sort of thing."

Brady would be attending a birthday party, she recalled. "Perfect. I'm free from two to four."

He tapped in a note. Putting her on the schedule, along with his dry cleaning and housekeeping service, no doubt.

Well, fine. This certainly wasn't a date. "We can practice breathing, too," Kate blurted.

"Oh?" He cocked an eyebrow. "Are you having trouble with that?"

Yes, but she hoped he hadn't noticed. "I mean, for childbirth!"

"Right." He put away the phone. "See you Saturday, then."

"See you."

The funny thing was, she noted after she closed the door quietly behind him, her house didn't feel cozy anymore. Without Tony, it felt kind of empty.

As Kate went to put away the cookies, she wondered if it was a mistake to spend more time with him. But since he had no close family, she seemed the logical person to help prepare him for his new role.

Neither of them was in any emotional state to begin a new relationship. As long as she kept that in mind, she should be fine.

Chapter Five

Like other members of the hospital staff, Tony had trained and prepared for disasters. Although Safe Harbor didn't operate an emergency room, its personnel were ready to pick up the slack should the region be shaken by a major earthquake or hit by a terrorist attack.

The following Wednesday's catastrophe, however, started with a simple Internet video featuring Dr. Samantha Forrest, the head of the hospital's pediatrics department. When not busy with patients or departmental duties, Samantha was setting up a low-cost counseling clinic for needy women and families in a spare office just down the hall from the administration suite.

"Jennifer called to alert us," Mark Rayburn explained around 4 p.m. after summoning Tony into his office. Jennifer Serra, the hospital's public relations director, was honeymooning in Hawaii with her groom, online news reporter Ian Martin. "Neither of them expected Flash News/Global"—Ian's employer—"to edit the interview in a sensationalistic way. She figured we'd better prepare for the public's reaction."

"To what, exactly?"

"I'll show you in a moment."

"I thought Ian was getting out of the news business. Isn't he writing a book about pregnancy issues?" Tony had hoped never to see another of the man's articles or videos about the hospital. They'd caused more than enough trouble already.

"He is. This was supposed to be his last interview." Mark clicked to a bookmarked Web site. "Actually, he did it as a favor to help raise funds for the Edward Serra Memorial Clinic." That was Samantha's counseling center, named for a baby Jennifer Serra had lost years earlier. "He squeezed in the interview right before the wedding. Damn! I clicked the wrong link."

Tony reined in his impatience. No sense venting his short temper on his perpetually tech-challenged boss.

He'd felt grumpy since last Friday, when Esther had arrived unexpectedly to file paperwork for their divorce, pack belongings and nag him to get a loan against the house. She'd stayed until Sunday, forcing him to cancel his session with Kate.

He'd hated calling it off, especially since he was trying to show what a reliable dad he would be. Tony hoped this nonsense on the Internet wasn't going to make him late for tonight's childbirth class. He'd vowed to be one of the first to arrive.

Finally Mark got the video started. "Here we go."

On screen, the suave Ian stood beside the tall blond pediatrician in an empty office. "I'm Ian Martin for Flash News/Global, reporting from Safe Harbor Medical Center. With me is Dr. Samantha Forrest."

"I'm thrilled that we're establishing a clinic to support families in crisis, especially young mothers who surrender their babies," Samantha said. "But as you can see, all we've got so far is space. We need funds for furniture, staff, computers—you name it."

"Was it really necessary to mention the babies?" Tony grumbled. "That's practically inviting another influx of kids. Social Services barely found enough homes for the last group."

"It's a smart tactic—donors take out their wallets for babies," Mark pointed out.

In the video, Ian regarded his subject encouragingly. "If Dr. Samantha Forrest had a magic wand—or perhaps a few very generous sponsors—what's her dream for the Edward Serra Memorial Clinic?"

The pediatrician's expression brightened. "Well…" An obvious editing cut skipped over what had probably been a list of services. The interview jumped ahead to "…those young ladies might come in feeling like Cinderella, but they'd leave feeling like princesses."

Mark's teeth made a grinding noise.

"Cinderella?" Tony said in disbelief.

"Princesses," the administrator muttered as if it were a dirty word.

"You'd buy them ball gowns?" Ian suggested on-screen. "Send them forth in carriages with white horses?"

"We'd give these girls a fresh start," Samantha enthused. "Career counseling, beauty makeovers, whatever they need. These young women who generously make the choice to give life should be featured on magazine covers instead of those overexposed TV stars."

"You heard it here first." Ian spoke directly to the camera. "Sexy Cinderellas, coming up!"

As the video ended, Tony felt a sudden urge to bang his head against the wall. "Don't they realize some people will take her literally?"

"You know Sam. When she's on a roll, there's no stopping her." Mark sounded pulled between admiration and annoyance.

"And Ian ought to know better!"

"Jennifer said he apologized. He got carried away—old

habits." The administrator shook his head. "As you may have heard, we had two relinquishments already today, and this was posted just yesterday."

"Yes, but there was nothing unusual about them, was there?" Even before Ian's previous reports created the wrong kind of publicity for the hospital, a few infants had arrived each month. Grateful that they weren't abandoned in dangerous circumstances, Tony had always been glad to help the young mothers fill out paperwork to free the babies for adoption.

"One of the girls got upset when she found out we don't offer makeovers," the administrator explained. "I'm afraid someone might sue us for false advertising."

Great. "We have to run damage control," Tony agreed.

"My thought exactly."

Naturally, disaster *would* strike while the PR director was out of town. Of course, since her husband had helped provoke it, her presence might have been a mixed blessing.

At Tony's suggestion, Mark called a meeting with Samantha, assistant PR director Willa Lightner and Betsy Raditch, the director of nursing. Sitting around a conference table, the five of them debated strategies and decided against holding a press conference, which was likely to call even more attention to the matter.

"We have to talk straight with the mothers," Tony insisted. "This is a hospital, not a reality show. Honesty is the best policy, and the more up-front we are, the less room for misunderstanding."

"I hate sending them off with nothing but a boot in the butt!" Dr. Forrest responded. Despite Tony's respect for the hardworking pediatrician, he wondered if she'd ever learn to guard her tongue. "I wish we had the staff to start counseling them right now. Some of our nurses have told me how much they sympathize. Maybe they'd be willing to pitch in."

"Their first obligation is to their patients," Betsy pointed out. "If they want to volunteer, that's fine, but most of them have family responsibilities on top of working their shifts."

"What about peer counseling?" Willa asked. "You don't have to be a psychologist or a nurse to listen and give advice."

"Peer counseling would be cost-effective," Mark agreed.

"Yes, but counselors have to be screened. Still, I'll keep that in mind." Samantha jotted a note.

"Now let's draft a simple, clear statement for our staff in case any more moms come in asking for makeovers," Tony said.

It was after six when they finished. That left him under an hour to grab dinner and change into the jeans he had brought.

Still plenty of time to get ready and arrive at class a few minutes early. Cheerfully, he headed for the cafeteria.

ON A BLANK WALL in the auditorium, Tina Torres's laptop projected the words *Labor, Contractions, Relaxation* and *Pain Management*.

How about anger management? Kate wondered. It was five past seven, the hum of conversation was dying down, and Tony still hadn't arrived.

She understood why he'd canceled their Saturday meeting, and besides, she wouldn't have enjoyed visiting his house with Esther around. Still, he'd been awfully cavalier about suggesting they reschedule for next weekend.

He didn't seem to realize that meant finding a sitter for Brady.

Now Tony was late again. How embarrassing to be the only woman sitting alone two weeks in a row.

Kate's sister had been skeptical about the prospects for daddy training. "Men have no idea how hard it is to manage a household and supervise kids," she'd griped this morning when Kate visited. "Even now that the boys are school age, there's PTA meetings and homework and running around buying supplies for special projects. Does the great attorney plan to leave all that to the nanny?"

"I don't get a say in how he raises Tara," Kate had responded as she helped fold laundry. Considering how often her sister helped *her,* it seemed only fair to assist with chores occasionally while Brady was in school.

"You have a moral obligation to your daughter!" Mary Beth had insisted.

"That isn't how our contract sees it. Besides, he'll come through. I'm sure he will."

As Tina went to close the auditorium door, Kate wished she were more certain of that. She supposed she could call Tony's cell number, but he shouldn't need reminding of his appointments.

Was that all fatherhood meant to him? Just another item on his calendar?

"Goodness." Tina hesitated in the doorway. "There seems to be a lot of commotion in the lobby. Wait!" She held up a hand as several attendees started to rise. "Whatever's going on, I'm sure it'll blow over by the time we're done here."

What kind of commotion? Regardless of whether it concerned Tony, Kate couldn't bear to sit here another minute. She'd been through childbirth, for heaven's sake. It wasn't as if she needed someone to tell her about contractions.

Kate grabbed her oversize purse. "Sorry," she said to the instructor, and hurried out.

What a relief. It wasn't as if she *had* to attend childbirth class, anyway. If she flunked, what were they going to do, refuse to let her give birth?

In the hallway, she heard what sounded like a surge of voices from the direction of the lobby. Curious, Kate headed down the corridor and rounded a corner.

So many people milled around the lobby that, being a mere five foot three, she could only see the ones closest to her. Cameras flashed, and above the din a couple of girlish voices were arguing vehemently, although she couldn't tell with whom.

Nearby, she spotted Dr. Rayburn's nurse. "What's going on?" Kate asked.

"We've been overrun by Cinderella wannabes." Lori waved her arm warningly as a young man with a video-cam eyed Kate's baby bulge. "Leave her alone!" she commanded. "She's one of our regular patients."

"Sorry." The reporter, or perhaps simply a gawker, ducked away.

"This is because of Dr. Forrest's remarks?" Alerted by a friend of Mary Beth's who'd called while they were folding laundry, Kate had seen the video. "But most of these girls are still pregnant. They can't be relinquishing their babies *yet*."

Lori shrugged. "I don't understand it, either. I popped over here to meet my fiancé for dinner, but he's busy trying to help sort out this mess."

When she pointed, Kate made out Dr. Jared Sellers, his head and shoulders visible above the throng. Oh! Nearby stood Tony, holding up a hand for quiet.

Glimpsing his expression of strained patience, she instantly forgave him for missing the class. And tried to ignore the inner voice whispering, *What about Tara? How many times will she have to forgive her only parent for missing her life?*

It wasn't as if he had a choice.

"Ladies!" he said. "Our administrator, Dr. Rayburn, and Dr. Forrest are on their way. They'll be happy to talk to you. However, there seems to be a misunderstanding about…"

"We understand just fine!" yelled a girl Kate couldn't see. "We're in the Moms-to-Be Club and we deserve makeovers just as much as those girls who give up their babies."

"Yeah!"

"You tell 'em!"

"That's right!"

More cameras flashed and whirred.

"Our assistant public-relations director, Mrs. Lightner, will take your names and contact information." Tony indicated a middle-aged woman with a pleasant face. "We'll do our best to help each of you with your particular situation."

"Here's my situation!" cried a girl, and with both hands, she extended her overgrown mane of frizzy hair.

"Shame on them," Lori said close to Kate's ear. "Don't they care about anything but their looks?"

"Who are they, anyway?" Kate could barely make herself heard over the hubbub.

"A group of unmarried teens that Dr. Forrest advises at a community center," Lori replied. "They showed up about fifteen minutes ago with the press in tow, demanding their so-called rights."

The noise around them eased as Dr. Forrest marched through the front door, parting the crowd as if she were a biblical figure. "Get a grip!" the pediatrician roared into the relative calm.

"Those of you who haven't lined up, please get in the queue so we can assess your needs," Tony added.

"I need to be beautiful and famous!" declared the frizzy-haired girl.

"What you need is a reality check," Dr. Forrest shot back. "You're about to become mothers, all of you. Are these your values—gimme gimme gimme? Now line up in front of Mrs. Lightner. You'll be contacted for an appointment."

"What kind of appointment?" called a man with a camera. "Beauty or counseling?"

"We'll figure that out when we get there." As the babble increased again, Samantha bellowed, "This is a hospital! There are people here waiting for loved ones in surgery! You girls show some common decency or I'll pitch every one of you out on your ears!"

In the shocked stillness, Kate noticed Tony's grim exchange of glances with Dr. Rayburn, who'd just arrived. They might not like the circus atmosphere, but the pediatrician's thundering apparently didn't go over so well, either.

In any case, the threat had the desired effect, because the girls lined up as requested. Surrounded by reporters, Dr. Rayburn patiently answered questions, somehow keeping calm despite the microphones thrust rudely in his face.

Kate slipped through the crowd until she reached Tony. "Hi."

Guilt flashed in his green eyes. "I'm late, aren't I?"

"Don't worry. I know more than I want to about contractions," Kate assured him.

"I hate disappointing you again," he said.

"I'm not disappointed. This is quite a situation—" Kate

broke off as Dr. Forrest joined them. A longtime client at Kate's salon, Samantha was the doctor who'd introduced her to the Francos in the first place.

While the pediatrician was conferring with Tony, Kate noticed a young blonde woman about five or six months along. Unlike the other girls, she stood alone, peering anxiously toward Tony and Samantha.

Kate made her way through the crowd, which was beginning to thin out. "Can I help you?" she asked.

"I'm not sure." The girl ducked her head, but not before Kate glimpsed a bruise on her cheek. If she was being abused, the police ought to be called, but that might frighten her away. Intuition warned that it was important to establish a connection first.

"My name's Kate," she went on. "I'm pretty good friends with some of the staff. What can we do to help you?"

"I didn't come here for some silly makeover," the young woman blurted.

"I'm sure you didn't." Kate waited while the girl fidgeted. "Someone hurt you, huh?"

A shrug. "My boyfriend's in jail, like he deserves."

"Are you considering giving up your baby?"

"No!" The girl's chin came up fiercely. "I want to *keep* my baby, not give it away." Her gaze fixed on Kate's abdomen. "I guess you'd understand."

Thank goodness she didn't know about the surrogacy. Kate disliked deceiving the girl, but she had to make the most of this rapport. "I think it's great that you plan to raise your baby. What's your name?"

"Eve."

The girl held on to the back of a couch as if taking strength from its bulk. "You seriously think these people will help me?"

"Yes. I'll walk over with you, if you like."

After a moment, the girl said, "Okay."

Kate introduced her to Tony and Samantha, and learned her full name: Eve Benedict.

On hearing the girl's circumstances, the pediatrician shifted gears. Where she'd railed at the superficial demands of the other girls, she took Eve under her wing, sympathetically collecting background information and promising to meet with her the next morning.

Tony drew Kate aside. "That was sweet of you."

"I didn't do much." Impulsively, she added, "But I'd like to. Do you suppose they could use my help at the clinic?"

He studied her thoughtfully. "You'd make a wonderful peer counselor."

"Really?" She hadn't expected to do more than handle paperwork. "Without a degree or anything?"

"That's what a peer counselor is," he explained. "Someone whose life experience helps them relate to the client."

"I'd like that."

After Eve left, Samantha seized on the suggestion. "Any chance you could come by tomorrow around 10 a.m.? I'd like you to help me work with Eve. She seems to trust you."

"I'd love to."

Dr. Rayburn was calling for Tony.

"Have a seat," he told Kate. "I'll be back as soon as I can. Unless you'd rather I meet you in class—what's left of it."

She had no desire to practice breathing. "I'll wait here."

Perched on a chair, Kate watched order restored to the lobby as girls and reporters drifted away. Peer counselor. That sounded exciting and rewarding. Plus, she'd been worried that her fellow nursing students might be far ahead of her in their studies. A volunteer post like this could be quite a confidence builder and looked good on her application.

Finally, Tony returned. "We're squared away for tonight," he said. "What can I do to make up for missing class?"

Give me a backrub. Hold me close. Do all the things a husband does when his wife is carrying a baby.

Alarmed at her response, she pushed those thoughts aside. "It's not as if you chose to stage Cinderella's ball in the lobby."

His appreciative grin sent tingles through her. Kate wished she could stay and talk, but she needed to release the sitter. "Walk you to your car?" he asked.

"Sure."

Taking her hand, Tony tucked it through the crook of his arm. "I wouldn't want to risk you falling in the dark."

People might talk. But right now, Kate didn't care.

They exited toward the garage. Outside, bright streetlamps pierced the darkness. The October breeze felt refreshing rather than chilly, probably because Kate's pregnant body radiated heat.

"I'm glad I can help at the clinic," she said as they walked. "I'm a little intimidated about starting back to college next semester after being out of school for so long. This might ease the transition."

"What're you planning to study?" He matched his pace to her slow gait.

"I thought I mentioned I'm going to nursing school."

He ducked his head ruefully. "You did. It slipped my mind. Are you sure you want to work in a madhouse like this?"

"I love the hospital. Plus, I've always enjoyed nurturing people." She'd be proud to have R.N. after her name.

"Nurses work incredibly hard." Tony helped her down the front steps.

"I understand it isn't all taking pulses and plumping pillows." She'd done her research. "You have to learn about everything from pharmaceuticals to trauma. But you're also the patient's first line of defense in getting proper care. I think good nursing is essential to healing."

"There isn't much glory," Tony warned. "As for the financial side, it's barely adequate."

In other words, her career would pale next to Esther's, Kate reflected. "I'm not in it for the glory."

"What about the money?"

"As long as I can pay my bills, I'm happy."

"I see."

Embarrassed, she realized how lame that must sound after he'd spent the weekend with his wife. Probably Esther had dazzled him with stories about the glamorous world of Washington and the earthshaking cases she was handling. So far, he hadn't mentioned a reconciliation, but he'd made it clear he wanted one.

"How did... I mean, did things go well last weekend?" Not wanting to seem nosy, she added, "Did Esther say anything about the baby?"

"She's glad it's a girl." He frowned at a burned-out light near the garage entrance and muttered, "Have to get that fixed. Can't have people falling in the dark."

Kate drew the subject back to his wife. "You mean she plans to stay involved?"

"With the baby? Not that she mentioned."

"Then why is she glad it's a girl?"

"I'm not sure." They stopped at Kate's battered car. "This is yours?"

"It's old but it runs." *More often than not.*

"Practically a classic." After that polite response, Tony waited while she keyed open the lock.

"Twenty years doesn't qualify it as a classic, I'm afraid." Besides, this particular model lacked any distinction. "My husband liked tinkering with jalopies."

"It has a certain raffish charm," he volunteered gamely.

"You're a bad liar, but a good diplomat." Well, it was getting late, and the babysitter had school tomorrow. "Thanks for seeing me off."

"You aren't off yet," Tony reminded her, and stepped back. "I'll wait till you get it started."

"This beast may be decrepit, but it's reliable." Now why had she said that? Pride, Kate supposed.

And pride, as she should have remembered, goeth before a fall. Or, in this case, it wenteth before a dead ignition.

Because when she turned the key, all she got was a click.

Chapter Six

A dead car. *Hey, great*, Tony thought. *Something I can fix.*

Well, not literally. He lacked her late husband's automotive skills. But he could arrange to get this fixed, unlike almost every other aspect of his world.

Last weekend, his attempts to talk Esther into marital counseling had scored a big zero. Caught up in her usual headlong rush, she'd wanted the divorce concluded yesterday, or the day before if possible.

"By next spring, we'll both be single again," she'd assured him.

"I'm not sure that's doable." He'd meant that it shouldn't be doable. What about trying to save their commitment and the nearly five years they'd spent together?

But he'd signed the papers she thrust at him. As strongly as Tony believed in marriage, and despite his concern about his wife's dramatic change in plans, he couldn't sustain a relationship by himself.

Nor, it seemed, could he make much sense of events at the hospital. Hordes of pregnant teens demanding beauty makeovers? What on earth did that have to do with medical care *or* the law?

Then, despite his resolve, he'd missed the childbirth class. Much as he appreciated Kate's reassurances, he'd let her down. Worse, he'd let Tara down.

He was beginning to question how well he'd handle being a single dad. An infant couldn't breeze into the hospital lobby and ask about the reasons for his delay. She couldn't wait until his schedule cleared to receive the attention she needed.

He *had* to get a grip on this fatherhood business. In the meantime, here, at least, was a tangible problem that ought to be fixable.

Tony peered under the hood. He hoped Kate didn't guess that, unless he stumbled upon a possum gnawing on the battery, he had no idea how to diagnose the problem.

No possums. No obvious loose wires, either. Still, he didn't carry jumper cables in his trunk for nothing.

"Let's get it started," he told her as he retrieved the cables. "I'll follow you to my mechanic's place down the street. And don't worry about the bill. I'll take care of it."

"I'll pay," Kate protested.

"You came here to attend a childbirth class, remember?"

"Yes, but my car had problems long before tonight."

"You haven't used my offer of handyman services, so let me help this way," he countered. "I'll follow you to the garage and drive you home. Do you need a rental car tomorrow? I can set that up."

His rapid-fire offers seemed to catch her off guard. Or perhaps she was mentally reviewing tomorrow's schedule. In any event, Kate considered for a moment before responding.

"I can walk Brady to school, and there's a bus that runs from there to the hospital," she said. "I'm meeting Eve at the clinic, remember?"

"That's right." He enjoyed the fact that she'd be volunteering at the clinic down the hall from his office. "But you shouldn't have to ride the bus to do a good deed."

She held up her hands. "I can't keep accepting favors. It feels like I'm taking advantage of you."

"If you insist on repayment…you don't happen to have any more cookies, do you?" he asked with a flare of anticipation.

She laughed, a wonderful, free sound that echoed through the nearly empty garage. "I'm afraid not, but I have another idea."

"You don't have to repay me."

"Hush." Kate laid a gentle finger over his lips. "Quit arguing, you stubborn man." Looking embarrassed, she moved her hand away. "That was cheeky of me."

His skin hummed from the contact. "I don't mind."

While she got behind the wheel, Tony attached the cables. In a moment, the car was revved and ready to go.

He gave her directions to the garage, and followed. They dropped the key and a note, including both their phone numbers, through the slot. Tony had done the same with his own car more than once when it developed a problem at night or on a weekend, and Phil always came through.

Although Tony understood the adrenaline rush that Esther must get from living in a city like D.C., he much preferred Safe Harbor. Small towns were wonderful.

When they arrived at Kate's cheery lemon-and-cream-colored bungalow, a teenage girl in braces met them at the door. "He finally dozed off," she informed Kate.

"Any problems?"

The girl shook her head. "No. He's a sweetheart, as always."

Tony stifled his impulse to insist on paying, since Kate had said she didn't want to keep accepting gifts. As he watched her handle the transaction, he had to admit he'd given little thought to the arrangements she had to make for Brady's care,

How cavalierly he'd requested she provide daddy training. Man, he *did* have a lot to learn.

After the sitter left for her house down the block, Kate went to peek into her son's room. Over her shoulder, Tony saw a little figure snuggled beneath the covers, only his blond head visible against the pillow.

Kate's shoulders relaxed as she released a small sigh. Was she always so tense when she was out of her son's sight? That constant awareness of another person depending on you—that was going to be his responsibility soon, too.

For the next twenty years.

If she could handle this, so could he, Tony told himself. All the same, fatherhood was shaping up to be a much bigger challenge than he'd expected.

In the kitchen, Kate closed the hall door as well as the swinging door to the dining room. "Is this favor noisy?" Tony still didn't have a clue what she intended to do.

"Slightly." From a drawer, she retrieved a pair of electric clippers. "You, sir, need a haircut."

He felt the top of his head. The bush that sprang back testified to the weeks, or perhaps months, that had passed since he'd visited a barber.

"You don't have to...." he began.

"Down! Here." She indicated a chair. "Wait. First take a couple of phone books from the counter to sit on, so I don't have to bend over."

Amused by her unaccustomed bossiness, Tony complied. "I feel like a kid," he said as he took a position atop the thick books.

"Afraid I don't have a proper chair at home." Kate produced a barber's cape, which she fastened around his neck. "Don't worry. I'm used to cutting Brady's hair this way."

"I wasn't worried." Except about the excitement that stirred as she deftly ran a comb through his hair. Up and down, over and over, with brisk, practiced movements that tugged lightly at his scalp.

The pressure of her fingers...the intimacy of the contact...her heated feminine scent...far too arousing. Tony thanked goodness for the concealing cape.

When the clippers buzzed, he shut his eyes and gave in to the gentle sensations as Kate worked upward from his neck. If he had to yield control to her, he might as well enjoy it.

HIS HAIR was thicker and wirier than Quinn's had been, with cowlicks that challenged Kate to trim them. She focused on treating Tony like any other person whose hair she'd cut over the years.

But he wasn't.

Tonight, when Tony relieved her of the burden of dealing with that recalcitrant clunker, his concern had soothed her like a caress. On the ride over here, she'd felt an inappropriate urge to nestle against him.

Since losing her husband, Kate had steadfastly taken charge of all the details of life that she used to share with Quinn. Paying the bills. Planning for Brady's future. Maintaining the house and car. Tony's insistence on sharing her burden, even a small one like a dead ignition, made her feel safe and cared for again.

When she'd decided to cut his hair, Kate had intended simply to repay a debt and maintain the balance between them. Some balance. She loved the feel of his hair and the grainy masculine skin of his neck. Moving about, she couldn't avoid brushing her bulge against him, and that reminded her of what lay inside.

Their daughter. His baby.

She pictured the little girl curled in her arms in the delivery room, with Daddy smiling down at them. And Tony retrieving her from the hospital, strapping Tara into an infant seat and taking Kate home.

This was crazy. Even though their worlds had intersected because of the surrogacy, Kate mustn't lose sight of reality. Tony's type of woman was an ambitious attorney like Esther, not a hairdresser. A woman who wore power suits and radiated importance, not a scruffy mom who wasn't sure she'd survive her first semester in nursing school.

After Tara's birth, he was free to break off all contact, and probably would. The most Kate dared aim for was to walk away with enough money to make things easier for her and Brady, and with her dignity, and her heart, intact.

Carefully, she snipped around Tony's ears, following their well-shaped curve. Along the back of his neck, she crafted a smooth line. Last step: check his head from all angles for any hairs she'd missed. Oops. Thanks to a cowlick, one section needed extra attention from the front.

Intent on her work, she didn't notice how close her pregnancy-enlarged breasts came to Tony's face until she heard his sharp intake of breath. Cheeks flaming, Kate moved away quickly.

Let's both pretend that didn't happen.

"Done?" he asked when she switched off the clippers.

"See what you think." She handed him a mirror.

He angled it several ways. "Excellent."

Kate whisked off the cape. "I can clean up later."

"No way. Where's the vacuum?"

She showed him. Tony insisted she sit down and rest

while he restored the kitchen to order, painstakingly cleaning corners and, after unplugging the machine, removing hair from the brush.

"You act like you've done that before," she said as he tucked the accessories into the vacuum.

"Surprised?"

"Well, yes," she conceded.

He regarded her steadily. "I'll admit, my family used a cleaning service. Dad was a personal-injury attorney, so we weren't poor. But Mom had her hands full taking care of Tara, and I helped where I could. Which included spot-cleaning."

"Difficulties can bring families closer." She and Mary Beth had forged a stronger bond since their mother's heart attack.

He returned the machine to the closet. "Dad kept busy with work, maybe busier than he had to. He expected perfection of everyone, including himself. I'm not sure he ever adjusted to having a handicapped child."

"How sad." Her heart went out to the little girl who must have felt her father's distance keenly.

"As a big brother, I tried to make up for him." Tony washed his hands in the sink. "Not that I was around all that much, either. Dad expected me to get top grades and be the star of the debate club."

"My sister was the high achiever in our family when we were younger," Kate admitted. "Not that our parents pushed us." Her father had sold furniture for a department store until it went out of business, and her mother had worked as a sales clerk. They'd taken pride in Mary Beth's college degree, but had also admired Kate's skill as a beautician.

"There's just you and your sister, right?" Tony said.

She nodded. "You mentioned a brother?"

"Leo. He's the middle child, second son. Tough position." He dried his hands with a paper towel. "He got attention by stirring up trouble. Cutting school, sneaking cigarettes, ditching homework. Drove Dad crazy."

"Any serious trouble?"

"Nope. In fact, he's now an officer with the Safe Harbor Police Department," Tony said. "I wish we were closer, since he's my only relative, but we don't have much in common."

"What about holidays?" Kate asked. "Surely you don't spend those alone."

He leaned against the counter. "We used to go to Esther's parents' house. This will be my first season by myself. I haven't made any plans yet."

"You should join us for Thanksgiving at my sister's house," Kate said on impulse. "My family puts on a big spread." She'd enjoy sharing it with Tony, especially since he obviously loved good food.

"That's very kind, but I couldn't intrude." From his crisp tone, she realized he probably didn't want to get too involved with a family he'd soon have to leave behind.

"I understand." Besides, she'd spoken out of turn. Since the event was held at Mary Beth's, Kate shouldn't have invited anyone without checking with her sister first. Especially since her sister disapproved of the surrogacy arrangement. "You might want to think about creating your own holiday traditions when Tara gets older. Like taking her to Disneyland for the day." The Anaheim theme park lay a half hour's drive inland.

"Or we could adopt a turkey instead of cooking it, and raise eggs in the backyard," he joked.

Kate laughed. "That'll go over great with your neighbors."

"I wonder why you never hear of anyone eating turkey eggs."

"I'll bet they make really *huge* omelets," she said. "Now you've made me hungry. Hang on." From the pantry, she fetched a package of pretzels. "Want some?"

"They aren't chocolate-covered, by any chance?" he asked wistfully.

"I'm afraid not."

"I guess I can forgive you, this time. What do you say to eating in front of the TV?" Tony must have caught her perplexed look, because he added, "We ought to catch the news to see if the hospital's on it."

"Oh!" She'd almost forgotten the evening's excitement. "Sure."

Kate cleared a newspaper on the couch to make room. The two of them settled comfortably side by side, feet propped on the coffee table, glasses of orange juice ready to wash down the salty pretzels.

Tony flicked across several channels. Once he found a news broadcast, they waited through national and international events.

During a commercial, both of them reached into the pretzel bag at the same time. Hands touched, and stayed there. Her skin prickling deliciously, Kate leaned closer and felt Tony's breath tingle across her cheek.

"We have to be careful not to break the bag," he murmured. "How about I pull out first?"

"Taking all the pretzels?" Kate teased. "*I* should go first."

"Stubborn, aren't you?"

"I know my rights."

Inches separated their faces. Less than inches. His mouth skimmed hers, bringing a flood of longing. She missed being held, kissed, stroked. Wanted all those things from Tony. And judging by the way he turned toward her, his thumb grazing her jawline, he wanted them, too.

Around them, the room shimmered with possibilities. Brady was sleeping and they had their privacy.

Kate relaxed into his arms and kissed him again.

Chapter Seven

From the TV, a man's voice boomed, "Here was the scene tonight at Safe Harbor Medical Center, where hordes of young mothers-to-be showed up expecting free beauty makeovers."

"Damn!" Tony snapped to attention.

Kate sank back. Why did the newscast have to switch to local news *now?*

On screen, the hospital's lobby churned with visitors. The camera zeroed in on a figure in a white coat. "There's Samantha!" he said.

Tony turned up the volume as the doctor scolded her audience. "You're about to become mothers, all of you. Are these your values? Gimme gimme gimme? Now line up."

Tony winced. "Out of context, that doesn't sound good."

Gimme gimme gimme. She'd been acting greedy herself a minute ago, hadn't she? Kate thought. Taking what didn't belong to her...

...even if it had been freely shared.

On TV, the anchorwoman said, "Guess those young moms have to wait for their free makeup and hairdos. By the way, this same hospital saw an influx of surrendered babies last month."

Her associate nodded. "I understand they specialize in fertility and maternity care. Guess if you can't keep your baby, that's the place to take it."

"And you may get a beauty makeover in the bargain." The anchorwoman pasted on an even broader smile. "After the break, video of a dog that loves to jump off the high diving board! Don't go away."

Kate buried her face in her hands. "Now we're on a par with diving dogs?"

Tony clicked off the TV. "What's worse is they repeated all that nonsense. Now we'll be jammed with babies, moms seeking makeovers, babies seeking makeovers and moms seeking babies with or without makeovers." He shook his head.

She recalled her promise to help Eve in the morning. "I hope that doesn't mean I can't start peer counseling."

"No reason why not. As long as you don't mind seeing the administrative staff snapping at each other," he warned. "Mark's been patient with Samantha, but I can tell that's wearing thin."

"She does have a gift for putting her foot in her mouth," Kate observed. "On the other hand, she gets credit for steering me to you." Afraid he might misunderstand, she added, "And Esther." How humiliating if he thought she was assuming anything on the basis of one kiss.

As the silence lengthened, she could feel Tony thinking. Unlike Dr. Forrest, he tended to think carefully before he spoke. Perhaps a bit too carefully for her.

"I should apologize for what happened before we were interrupted," he began.

"No, you shouldn't."

"If I've given you the impression that I expect more than..."

He *did* think she was jumping to conclusions. "You

haven't given me any impression. I'm a sex-starved widow, that's all."

"Kate!" He looked startled.

"Tony, things happen," she persisted. "You're a good-looking man, I'm a single woman and my hormones are running amok. It doesn't mean anything." *I wish.*

He didn't seem convinced. "All the same, my suggestion that you come over and advise me about the nursery was unwise. I'm not saying we're too impulsive to be alone together, but I didn't take into account your babysitting issues. It's unfair to you."

"*And* we should probably avoid being alone together," she conceded.

Tony stretched. "It's getting late.'"

Kate tried to ignore the stiffness in her legs as she rose. "Thanks again for my car."

"No problem." As he ambled out, he said, "See you in the morning."

"By the way, nice haircut." She restrained the urge to fluff his hair as he went by.

"I have a talented hairdresser," he responded lightly.

"Anyone can trim a man's hair."

"If my wife tried, I'd be minus part of an ear," he corrected. "Possibly on purpose."

"You have nice ears." Kate bit her lip. "I didn't mean... I just see a lot of ears, in my business."

"And resist trimming them."

"Mostly."

He lingered on the porch, studying her. At last, he said a simple good-night and walked away.

What was wrong with her? Kate wondered as she closed the door behind him. Earlier, she'd practically propositioned the man, and then she'd started flirting again.

Okay, so she longed, for the first time in years, to feel a man's arms around her that weren't Quinn's.

Well, she couldn't go on acting like a teenager. From now on, she intended to behave herself around Tony.

No matter how hard that might be.

How COULD ONE KISS wreak such havoc on his emotions? Tony had trouble falling asleep, and woke from a dream that—well, if there were a way to capture that kind of dream for replay, he'd be in all kinds of trouble.

He had to get past this. Even if he weren't still married, he couldn't ignore the fact that he'd contracted with Kate to bear his child. Before entering into the agreement, Tony had researched cases involving surrogacy, so he knew the pitfalls if the woman didn't fully accept her obligation to relinquish all rights. Moreover, at his previous job with a family-law firm, he'd seen ugly child-custody battles between spouses that dragged on for years. They benefited no one except the law partners, who earned enough to buy yachts and vacation homes.

No matter how strongly Tony might be tempted to get closer to Kate, he would never risk landing in that kind of mess. And much as he'd like Tara to have a relationship with her mother, this situation required clear boundaries.

Giving up on sleep, he swam laps in his pool, then worked out in his home gym to release his excess energy. A shower and fresh clothes helped him get into the right mindset for what was sure to be a difficult day.

He arrived at the medical center early, but not early enough to beat the press. Several reporters and a camera crew clustered in the lobby, talking to a dark-haired young woman whose professional demeanor failed to mask her aura of happiness.

Public relations director Jennifer Serra excused herself

and took Tony aside. "The news traveled all the way to Hawaii. Ian and I decided to come back early."

"Too bad about your honeymoon, but I have to admit, it's great to see you," he said. "How's it going so far this morning?"

"Two babies came in during the last hour," she told him. "Samantha's meeting with the moms upstairs in the clinic."

"I'm on it."

The new clinic certainly was being pressed into service, Tony mused as he reached the fifth floor and found the young women filling out their forms. Ironic, considering that the place didn't have any staff, permanent furniture or an official opening date yet.

Scarcely had those young moms departed when three more mothers and infants arrived. A camera crew sneaked onto the fifth floor via a rear entrance, and Mark—who'd ducked in from seeing patients at the medical building next door—had to draw Samantha out of camera range to make sure she didn't accidentally stir up another hornet's nest.

Mercifully, by nine o'clock, the crew had been banished, the babies entrusted to a social worker and both doctors freed to see patients. Peace returned to the clinic.

That lasted about five minutes.

Tony was straightening the folding chairs when Jennifer Serra popped in. Her strained expression warned of trouble, and sure enough, behind her trailed a half a dozen pregnant teenagers he recognized from the previous night. "Makeovers," she mouthed.

One girl addressed Tony. "We lined up and left our names the way you told us. Nobody called."

"Since last night?" he asked, astonished by her impatience. "Some of us sleep, you know."

The publicity director took him aside. "For the instant-messaging generation, patience isn't a long suit." As he shook his head in disbelief, she added, "I've got the press salivating downstairs, and if we don't come up with something fast, these girls are threatening to stage their own reality show in the lobby."

Despite Jennifer's attempt to keep her voice down, the leader of the pack stuck her nose into the conversation. "Yeah. You better make us beautiful or we'll tell those TV guys what a rip-off this is."

"I disagree about who's getting ripped off here," Tony responded. "As for your threats…" Damn. It wasn't like him to go off half-cocked. He took a deep breath. "I'm sure we can find a reasonable solution."

"Yeah, maybe." The girl retreated, her expression smoldering.

"I leave it to you, counselor. You have my sympathy." Jennifer caught sight of Jared in the hallway. "Oh, good, here's Dr. Sellers. I'll steer him downstairs to tell the press what's involved in treating babies born without proper medical care. That'll hold them for a while." And off she went, snagging the neonatologist and leaving Tony alone with a roomful of surly teenagers.

He bristled as yet another pregnant woman sauntered through the door. Then her golden-brown gaze met his. Kate! Relief and a spark of hope replaced his irritation.

The girls regarded her as if unsure what to make of this new, older arrival with an abdomen to match theirs. "Hey," Kate greeted the group, then made her way around to Tony. "What gives?"

"I seem to be stuck with the makeover madonnas," he grumbled. "Any ideas?"

She turned to study the girls. "What exactly do you have in mind?" she asked them.

"Hair!" The frizzy girl extended her locks, mirroring her actions of the previous night.

"Makeup!" declared a chubby teen without bothering to remove a licorice stick from her mouth.

"Somebody to fix me up so I can get a job after the baby's born," said a pretty African-American girl who'd dyed her hair orange.

"I'll see what I can do." Kate pressed a key on her cell phone. "Good thing I work at a salon, isn't it?"

Tony could have hugged her, but the idea reawakened a host of impulses and a tantalizing memory of last night's dream. To hide his reaction, he concentrated on scowling at the madonnas.

"Hi, it's Kate," she said into the phone. "Are you guys busy this morning? How'd you like to do some makeovers and get tons of press coverage?"

Now why hadn't he considered the publicity angle? Not only was Kate relieving the hospital of the young moms, she might distract the ravening reporters, as well.

"Half a dozen," Kate continued, apparently answering a question about the number of girls. "Mostly cuts and highlights, a color correction, some curl relaxing. Makeup to wear on job interviews. Sure, nails would be great if someone's available. Wonderful. I'll send them right over." She clicked off.

"Did I ever mention that you're a genius?" Tony asked.

"It's a win-win for everybody." Kate produced a sheaf of business cards, which she distributed among the girls. While she provided driving directions, Tony phoned Jennifer so she could tip off the press.

"I'll go, too," the PR director said. "We have to be careful not to give the impression we'll do this for everyone. I'll point out that this is a goodwill gesture by the salon."

"Perfect."

Faster than Tony would have believed possible, the clinic emptied out. All that remained of the girls were the scents of bubble gum and licorice.

"What a relief," he said. "Thank you."

Kate chuckled. "That was fun."

"Fun?"

"Did you see how thrilled they were? My colleagues will get a kick out of this. Not to mention the free publicity. It's good for the salon, and don't forget, I'll be working there again part-time after the baby's born." Kate dropped her purse on a chair. "Those girls are cute, aren't they?"

"When they're not threatening to embarrass the hospital." Tony plucked a piece of cereal from her sleeve. "Cornflakes?"

She squinched her nose in embarrassment. "I don't know how Brady manages to get them stuck all over himself *and* me."

"You walked him to school okay?"

A nod. "I should do that more often. Kids spend too much time riding in cars."

That reminded him of a call he'd received earlier. "My mechanic confirmed that he'll have your ignition switch fixed later this morning."

"That's wonderful." She lingered close enough for Tony to see another bit of cereal clinging to her shoulder, so he removed that, too. As he leaned close, the sudden rise and fall of her chest beneath the flowered blouse showed that she, too, was breathing harder than normal.

Dangerous territory.

"What's next, boss?" Kate murmured.

"I'm not your boss."

"You're the only one here," she pointed out. "I can't run the clinic myself."

"The clinic isn't open." He wished Samantha would finish with her patients.

"Coulda fooled me." As Kate studied the bare walls and empty inner offices, Tony could almost see her mentally furnishing it. "This place has possibilities. I'm not sure if Eve's going to make it this morning or not, but I could stick around in case other moms show up."

"That would be terrific, if it isn't too much work." He didn't want to overstress her. "Have you had any training?"

"Doctor Forrest was going to work with me this morning. But at least I can listen and sympathize." She reached into her large purse. "Besides, I brought an anatomy book to study."

"You mean we have homework from childbirth class?" Tony reached for the hefty blue volume. "May I see that?"

"Sure. And don't worry. I'm just getting a head start on college."

He thumbed through the book, noting the small type and detailed medical illustrations. "You take your nursing career seriously."

"I'm not entirely a nitwit."

Startled, he looked up. "Who said you were?"

She waved a hand. "Nobody."

"I don't assume you lack intellect because you're a hairdresser." He hadn't meant to imply any such thing.

"I don't even have a B.A."

"Neither did Shakespeare."

"I never thought of it that way." She accepted the book back. "Just imagine what he could have accomplished if he'd had an education."

They both laughed. "Anyway, if you're going to be doing some counseling it's a given that studying alone can't make anyone an expert," Tony mused. "A good therapist draws on life experience. So does a good lawyer or doctor."

"My dad used to say people can be too smart for their own good," Kate agreed. "They assume they can solve any problem just by thinking about it. Whereas really smart people, well, I guess they're willing to admit how much they *don't* know. Which I guess makes me a genius, because I'm willing to admit I know hardly anything."

Tony had to think about that one for a minute. "I'll vote for you being a genius," he concluded.

She grinned. "Thanks."

He wished he could stick around longer, but by now his computer must be flashing with messages. "If you'll stop by my office when you're done, I'll fix you a cup of coffee. Or decaf, if you prefer."

"Sounds good. I've cut back on caffeine for the duration." She settled on a chair and propped the book on her knees, in lieu of a lap. "Meanwhile, I'll amuse myself memorizing parts of the digestive system."

He peered over her shoulder. "Doesn't that diagram give you indigestion?"

She patted her bulge. "With all this pressure, everything gives me indigestion. But it's worth it."

Tony could have sworn he spotted another cornflake on her temple, begging to be removed. And sitting so close to an air conditioning vent, she might be cold. He ought to offer her his jacket.

Pregnant women are never cold. And you've got work to do.

With a quick, "See you later," Tony tore himself away. Because if he didn't go now, he might never leave.

KATE TRIED TO CONCENTRATE on the strange anatomical terms. Cecum, jejunum, ileum. That last one sounded like an ancient Greek epic.

She couldn't stop thinking about Tony touching her as he removed those silly cornflakes. Her blood glimmered through her veins like silver as she imagined running her hands over him, too.

You idiot.

Last night, he'd made it plain that he intended to keep his distance. True, he'd just invited her for coffee, but only in a safe business setting.

She'd never felt such confusion with Quinn. From the start, their relationship had been straightforward and relaxed. Sure, there'd been a few simmering issues, such as her concern about his risk-taking and the way he never managed to save money, but she'd figured he'd grow out of those tendencies.

Well, she'd better outgrow her tendency to daydream. Kate returned to her book, and was deep in the intricacies of the ascending, descending and transverse colon when a movement drew her attention to the entrance.

Eve's bruised cheek had gone from dark red to yellowish brown. A small pucker formed between her eyebrows as she surveyed the room.

"Good morning." Kate set the book aside.

"Are...are you a counselor?"

She should have called Dr. Forrest, Kate reflected, but she hadn't been sure Eve would really come. "I'm a peer counselor. Let's talk about your situation, and maybe I can help you figure out the next step."

"Yeah?" The girl edged into a chair. "How old are you, anyway?"

"Twenty-seven. How about you?"

"Nineteen." A deep breath. "Somebody told me you were a surrogate."

Kate had been wondering how to break the news. "That's right."

"What's it like?"

Kate explained briefly, and at last Eve unbent enough to talk about herself. Although she had a part-time job at a discount store, it didn't pay enough to support her, let alone a child. Her father, an alcoholic, had abandoned the family long ago, and her mother, who lived out-of-state with a second family, would only take Eve if she agreed to serve as an unpaid housekeeper.

"I depended on Duane, which was really dumb. He used to beat up his old girlfriend. I never thought he'd do it to me."

"He's in jail, right?"

"Yeah, but I can't pay my rent without his help. It's like nobody cares if I die in the street!" the mom-to-be burst out.

"I care," Kate reminded her.

"I can't get welfare because I have a job, but if I give up my job, I might never find another one. It's not fair."

"Instead of complaining, let's do some planning," Kate suggested. "We should assess your strengths and figure out what steps you can take to make things better."

"That's easy for you to say," Eve grumbled. "You've got a nice cushy life."

The resentful tone brought Kate up short. "What makes you think that?"

"Well, it's obvious. I mean…" The girl searched for justification. "You're being paid to carry somebody's baby. That makes you rich, right?"

"I'm a widow with a five-year-old son, and right now I'm too big to work at my regular job as a hairdresser."

Kate paused just long enough for her words to sink in. "These past two years since my husband died have been a struggle."

"I'll bet you have family you can lean on," the girl countered.

"I try not to lean on them too much."

"Yeah, but you can if you have to."

Eve's whining struck a nerve. "You're about to become responsible for another person's life. Sure, things are tough right now, but being angry at the world won't solve your problems. And neither, in the long run, will anybody else. If you plan to keep this baby, you have to grow up fast."

As soon as the words were out, Kate felt a pang of apprehension. She was supposed to help Eve, not antagonize her.

"You're saying I should give up my baby?" The teenager glared at her. "I'll never let him go, never."

Her loud voice must have disturbed Tara, who chose that moment to start practicing her soccer kick. Kate's hand flew to her abdomen. As she registered her daughter's activity, the irony of Eve's words hit home. *Why am I lecturing her? She's braver than I am.* "Good for you. I'm glad you're sticking by your baby."

"Yeah, sure. You're just like everybody else. You think I'm a screwup."

"No, I don't." Kate blinked back a film of tears. "The thing is, from now on, you're in charge of your life *and* his. Not your mother, not your boyfriend, not your friends or relatives and not me. How much are you willing to sacrifice to keep him?"

Eve folded her arms. "Why should I have to sacrifice anything?"

"Because sacrifice goes along with parenthood, especially single parenthood." Kate was glad to see the girl listening intently. "You need to find a stable situation, even if that means moving in with your mother for a while and living by her rules."

"I hate her. We fight all the time."

"Well, somehow, you have to find a solution, and you have to keep finding solutions for the next twenty years," Kate emphasized. "Stop making excuses and let me help you look for answers."

Judging by the girl's mutinous expression, this discussion had gone too far. "You want me to grow up? Fine. I sure don't need you!"

"I didn't mean it that way." Too late. The girl was storming out of the room, too fast for Kate to follow. "Eve!"

No response. Kate sat stunned. Her first attempt as a counselor, and she'd failed.

Guiltily, she wondered if she should simply leave and not return. With no formal organization yet, the clinic wouldn't miss her, and she could always make some vague excuse to Samantha later.

But she'd promised to have coffee with Tony. Besides, sneaking off didn't feel right.

She was going to have to admit her failure. More than that, the conversation had stirred emotions that Kate had been trying very hard to ignore. Feelings about her own baby and her own decision.

What if Mary Beth was right? What if this whole arrangement had been a terrible mistake?

She'd promised to bear a child for the Francos. But she'd done so in the belief that her child would have a loving father *and* mother.

In the week since she'd learned of Esther's departure, Kate hadn't allowed herself to fully consider the implications. Now, Eve's passionate commitment to her child had splashed cold water in her face.

Kate couldn't simply go on pretending things were fine. She had to share her doubts with someone.

And that someone, like it or not, should be Tony.

Chapter Eight

Although it wasn't a requirement of the job, Tony believed in keeping informal tabs on the medical center's departments by dropping in on them. That way, staff could ask questions and alert him to potential problems.

In addition, since his arrival three years ago until last month's official reopening, he'd suffered through almost nonstop remodeling work on what had been an aging community hospital. Now he enjoyed touring the state-of-the-art facilities that served primarily women and newborns.

Today, Tony visited the third floor, home to the labor and delivery rooms and the regular- and medium-care nurseries. In L&D, the few nurses who weren't in a rush asked him about dealing with the reporters who sometimes sneaked onto their floors.

"Never answer questions without first consulting the public relations office," he told them. "If they persist, don't hesitate to call security. We have an obligation to protect patient privacy."

"What if a patient *wants* to give an interview?" asked a male nurse.

"A patient can't give informed consent while medicated," Tony warned. "Our policy is that if patients wish to talk to the press, they should do so after they're discharged, or at least with next of kin *and* a member of the hospital administrative staff present."

A young man rushed past, bumping Tony's shoulder. "Sorry, my wife's in labor," he called without stopping.

"Understood."

A nurse cast Tony a knowing smile. "That'll be you soon, won't it?"

"I'm sorry?"

"I heard you were coaching the surrogate. Too bad your wife flaked out." Her face scrunched. "Oops. Didn't mean to meddle."

"I *am* learning to be her labor coach," he confirmed. At least, that was the idea. He really had to stop missing classes.

To discourage any further personal remarks, Tony said a friendly farewell and headed to the hallway. He should have realized that his personal situation had become fodder for the grapevine. Hospitals were hotbeds of gossip.

Which meant, Tony reflected, that every time he talked to Kate in the lobby or any other public area, the staff would be nattering about it the next day. If that didn't make a guy self-conscious, he wasn't sure what would. Yet he refused to stop coaching her, no matter how much close contact that involved. Or how many tongues wagged as a result.

As he passed the nursery, he couldn't resist pausing at the display window. Back when Esther was trying to get pregnant, he used to come here almost daily, fantasizing that one of those little sweethearts belonged to them.

There hadn't been any reason to believe Esther was infertile, aside from irregular menstrual periods, which she'd attributed to her high-pressure schedule. But after months of trying in vain, they'd submitted to a series of tests. Roughly a year ago, they'd sat in Mark's office, stunned as he explained the diagnosis.

Esther had premature ovarian failure, which, he'd told them, meant a problem with the ovarian follicles, the seeds that matured into eggs. For unknown reasons, she'd suffered what the doctor termed follicle depletion, meaning that she had no follicles left and no way to grow more.

The only way for her to bear a child would be to undergo hormone treatments and receive an egg donation from another woman. This was a rigorous procedure, with the odds of success less than ten percent.

Esther had gone stone cold, barely speaking to Tony for several days despite his attempts to comfort her. When she proposed hiring a surrogate, he'd been relieved to see her animation return.

He'd almost forgotten her initial intention of hiring a university student, with the goal of producing a high-IQ child. After learning there weren't any available, she'd compromised on Kate.

Well, in Tony's opinion, Kate was both smart and very, very special. So what if she couldn't memorize case law and summon it with deadly precision in court? She understood what mattered in life, in a way that Esther probably never would.

Staring at the row after row of adorable babies, Tony reflected that, for years ahead, he was likely to be identifying Kate's characteristics in his daughter. The smile that blossomed from warm to mesmerizing, the eyes with their shadowed depths… No, that came from the loss she'd survived. He hoped his daughter never suffered such grief.

Had Esther stayed in the picture, Tony would never have thought much about what Kate had gone through. Now they'd formed an unexpected connection. Too bad it had to be temporary.

Or did it?

"Those twins were surrendered this morning." Stopping beside Tony at the window, Jared Sellers indicated babies in side-by-side bassinets. "While I was examining them, it surprised me how much they remind me of my sister's kids."

"Are you reconsidering your decision not to have children?" Tony had heard that Jared's fiancée, who'd grown up supervising five younger sisters, opposed becoming a mother.

The neonatologist's mouth twisted. "I never believed guys had biological clocks, but this feeling is *intense*. Lori's supposed to move in with me next week. She plans to turn the spare room into her office, and I'm imagining a nursery."

"You'd better discuss this with her, pronto," Tony advised. "I wish I'd communicated more with my wife." If Esther had confided her change of heart about having a child, they might have worked out a compromise and saved their marriage.

"Guess she and I do need to have a talk. Not looking forward to it." His beeper sounded. "Gotta go. Catch you later."

As Tony returned to the administrative suite, he spotted Kate hovering near his inner doorway. "Sorry to keep you waiting."

"That's okay. I know you're busy."

Aware of the secretary's curious gaze, Tony guided her into his office, his hand drifting to the small of Kate's back. Now why had he done that? He'd likely just stirred up a whole afternoon's worth of gossip.

"Coffee?" He kept a private pot stocked with his favorite blend. "Oh, that's right—too much caffeine. I can fix instant decaf."

"No, thanks. I'm not thirsty."

Instead of retreating behind his desk, Tony took a seat beside her. "What's wrong?"

Deep breath. "I'm afraid I'm a failure as a peer counselor."

Considering how brilliantly she'd handled the makeover moms, he doubted that. "What happened?"

She gripped her purse. "Eve started feeling sorry for herself and implying it was other people's responsibility to take care of her. I lectured her about how parents have to sacrifice for their children. Way too heavy-handed. No wonder she walked out."

Tony didn't know what advice to offer. Besides, her instincts were probably better than his. "If you had it to do over, what approach would you take?"

"I'd help her find a solution," Kate said glumly. "I was working around to that, but we never got there."

"Call her. Samantha must have the phone number."

A slow nod. "It's worth a try. I hope Dr. Forrest won't be mad."

"She asked you to assist with Eve, not run the show solo. She's the one at fault here. Besides, once Eve cools down, she might view things differently." Kate had a gift for relating to needy girls. Despite today's setback, in Tony's opinion, she'd make a fine peer counselor.

Also, he liked the idea of her showing up regularly at the clinic, just a few doors away. Although he'd resolved not to spend time alone with Kate, once a week in class hardly seemed like enough time to be around his developing baby.

As if the person he wanted to be close to was Tara. *You are treading a very fine line here, counselor.*

Exactly how fine struck him when he heard Kate's next words. "In some ways, Eve's a better mother than I am.

She's determined to keep her baby. Here I am, agreeing to bear a child for someone else and then walk away."

Tony stiffened. He'd allowed them to grow close, so close that he'd considered continuing the relationship after she gave birth, and now Kate felt free to question the surrogacy arrangement. He should have foreseen this.

He had to clarify the rules and return the situation to the right footing. The sooner the better.

"You'll *have* to walk away," he said more sharply than he'd intended. "That's the way it works, Kate."

At the pain in her startled gaze, his gut tightened. Too bad. Her statement had forced him to clamp down. The fact that he had only himself to blame merely added to his resolve.

Tony's sudden coldness chilled Kate. She'd spoken openly, trusting the sense of support between them. Confiding in him, not challenging their contract. Well, not exactly. She'd never expected him to turn hard and remote.

"I just figured we could discuss this." When he offered no reassurance, she rose awkwardly. "I'd better be going."

He stood, also. "I'm sorry if I've led you to believe there's any flexibility in our contract. It's very clear on the subject of custody."

"I'm aware of that," Kate said tightly.

"Second thoughts may be natural, but you should have considered all the issues before you signed those documents."

Was he *trying* to tick her off? "How can anyone consider all the issues? Seven months ago, you had no more idea than I did of how you'd feel at this point!"

"That's irrelevant."

Did he have to act like such a…such a *lawyer?* "What

if Tara confronts me someday and says, 'How could you abandon me and let me grow up without a mom?' What if she asks how *you* could keep her away from her mother? This isn't a house we contracted to build, it's a person! And she was supposed to have a mother."

His eyes narrowed. "If we're going to court over this, I assure you, I will win."

Kate bit off an angry reply. "Whether you'd win or not, you know perfectly well I can't afford to fight you," she said as steadily as she could. "All I'm asking is for you to consider our daughter's future happiness, the way I'm doing."

"I'll take care of my daughter's happiness," he said.

"Yes, you will," she answered, fighting tears. "You'll be a great dad. When you're around."

Rather than break down in front of him, she wrenched the door open and hurried out. On the way to the exit, Kate kept her head low to avoid meeting anyone's gaze.

Then she remembered that her car was still at the shop. Well, a short walk might relieve her frustration.

En route, she called Dr. Forrest. Rather than criticizing, the pediatrician took responsibility for failing to meet with Eve. "I got called away on a case, and it slipped my mind. Would you rather I phoned her, or do you want to?"

Kate might have no choice about relinquishing Tara, but she refused to give up on Eve. "I'll do it. What's her number?" She tapped it into her phone. "Thanks."

"Thank *you*," Samantha said. "See you again next Thursday? We may have other girls trickling in."

"I'll be there."

Before she lost her nerve, Kate pressed Eve's number. It rang several times and went to voice mail.

She identified herself and left her phone number. "I'm sorry about lecturing you. Please call me or drop by the clinic next Thursday morning. If you'd prefer to talk to Dr. Forrest, I can set that up."

At the garage, the mechanic, Phil, greeted her with the good news that he'd fixed the problem, and waved away Kate's offer to pay. "Mr. Franco took care of it. I, uh, heard about the surrogacy business. That's a brave thing you're doing."

She didn't feel very brave. "It's complicated."

"You're Quinn's widow, aren't you?"

She nodded.

"Your husband and I used to bail each other out when one of us got more business than we could handle. I was real sorry to hear about his accident. Anytime your car acts up, I'll throw in the labor for free."

His kindness loosened the tears she'd held back earlier. "That's very generous."

"Didn't mean to make you cry." He lifted the oily rag in his hand. "Oh, sorry. Not exactly a clean handkerchief, huh?"

Kate chuckled, and felt a little better. "I appreciate the impulse."

Phil handed her the key. "If you have any more problems, just call."

"Thanks." After repairing her makeup in the mirror, she started the car. It purred smoothly to life.

Heading toward Brady's school, she supposed she ought to send Tony a note of gratitude for the repair. Or she could tell him in person at next Wednesday's class—if he showed up.

How could a man be so sweet and yet so infuriating? Well, he'd certainly put her in her place today. *I guess to him I'm nothing more than the hired help.*

Forget the thank-you note.

Still, she'd chosen this role, hadn't she? Tony was right

about one thing. She should have weighed the issues more carefully before she signed the contract.

Kate forgot her turmoil the moment she spotted Brady's dear face among a knot of kindergarteners. She collected a big hug, along with a construction-paper art project covered with autumn leaves.

"Great job," she said, stowing the paper in the rear seat.

"Can I get a hamburger for lunch?"

"Sure, as a special treat. I'll have one, too." Although Kate didn't often eat fast food, she'd saved a two-for-one coupon from last Sunday's paper.

Afterward, Brady napped at home, and then they swung by her sister's house. Their mother was attending a knitting class at the senior center, but Kate had to talk to someone.

She joined Mary Beth on the patio. While they watched the kids play, Kate recounted the morning's events.

"Please don't say 'I told you so,'" she begged her sister. "It's not that I want to keep Tara, or that I regret having her, either. I only wish Tony would allow me some involvement, since Esther's out of the picture."

"What if he remarries?" Mary Beth asked. "Once the baby has a stepmother, he for sure won't want you around."

"I suppose that's true." A man as attractive as Tony wasn't likely to stay single forever. Sooner or later, he'd find another sophisticated, high-power woman to share his life.

"You should sue for joint custody," her sister continued. "Then he can't simply elbow you aside."

"I'm not suing anybody." Kate couldn't face that kind of disruption or expense, or the anguish of becoming Tony's enemy, which was probably how he'd view her. "I guess it's lucky he turned down my invitation to Thanksgiving dinner. That would have been awkward."

"Oh! About that." Mary Beth broke off to pick up a tot who'd tumbled to the grass. After a brief inspection revealed only a mild bruise, the little one scampered back to play and Mary Beth returned, dusting off her hands. "I meant to tell you. Ray has to work the afternoon shift on Thanksgiving."

Kate's brother-in-law often arrived late or left early on holidays. "We can eat early." They'd done that frequently.

"I'm tired of getting up at 3 a.m. to put a bird in the oven," her sister grumbled. "We've decided to postpone the big meal this year. Ray has the weekend off, so we'll fly to Lake Tahoe to visit his parents. They're fixing a turkey dinner on Saturday. Sorry to leave you in the lurch, but it works out better for us."

Although the news disappointed her, Kate understood. "You've done more than your share of holiday cooking. You deserve a break."

"We invited Mom to Tahoe, but she prefers staying here alone for a couple of days. She says she'll enjoy a little peace and quiet." Leaning back in a chaise, Mary Beth closed her eyes. "It'll be nice to have a holiday off."

Kate ought to take it easy for Thanksgiving, too. Brady might enjoy a restaurant dinner. But what kind of celebration would it be without a family gathering?

"I'll fix the meal at my house," she volunteered. "I can't get it ready early enough for Ray, but you and Mom and the kids should come." In view of Kate's pregnancy, surely no one would object to a few shortcuts such as paper plates and canned cranberry sauce.

"I don't expect you to do this!" her sister protested.

"Why not? I'm perfectly capable," Kate countered. "You may be four years older, but I'm a grown-up now, too."

The relief on Mary Beth's face was all the reward she could have asked for. "That sounds wonderful. I'll help, of course."

"No, you won't," Kate protested. "This is my treat. *All* of it. As long as you promise not to complain if I buy the pies instead of baking them."

"I won't breathe a word," her sister assured her. "Wow, baby sis, you *are* growing up."

"And out." Kate patted her belly.

"You wear it well."

Her mind flew ahead to the details of shopping and cooking. Preparing her first solo holiday meal was going to be challenging but fun.

Not nearly as much fun without Tony, whispered a rebellious voice. But then, this was likely to be Kate's only Thanksgiving with Tara. She intended to enjoy every precious moment.

Chapter Nine

Kate spent most of Friday drawing up a menu for Thanksgiving. Although she'd intended to simplify, she couldn't omit too many family favorites. Sausage-and-raisin stuffing. Baked fresh yams with marshmallow topping. But how could she bake the yams *and* the turkey with only one oven?

With careful planning, she decided. For one potential problem, though, she had no easy solution: the house's single bathroom. How inconvenient, in view of Brady's impatience and her own condition. Everyone would have to form a line and wait their turn. Hardly an earth-shattering dilemma.

That evening, after putting her son to bed, she started on the shopping list, consulting the recipes and trying to calculate how big a turkey to buy. Every year, she'd fixed a few dishes, but had never appreciated how much work her mother and then Mary Beth put into planning the event. Thank goodness she had nearly three weeks to get organized.

A wave of sleepiness overcame Kate as she sat on the couch. Thanks to pregnancy hormones, she felt suddenly too tired even to prepare for bed, so she simply leaned back and almost instantly fell asleep.

The shrill of the phone penetrated her sleep-fogged

mind. Uncertain how much time had passed, she groped for the phone and dragged it to her mouth. "Hello?"

"You have to help me!" The shaky female voice sounded young and scared.

On the point of asking who it was, Kate recalled leaving her number for Eve earlier. "Eve?"

"Duane nearly got me!"

Duane. The vicious ex-boyfriend. "Isn't he in jail?"

"They let him out. Can you believe it? He just showed up. I slammed the door, climbed out the window and ran. Couldn't even grab my purse. I'm outside some convenience store at a pay phone."

"Did you tell the police?"

"I'm standing here in my bathrobe!" Eve cried. "I can't deal with a bunch of cops, and anyway, this call used up all the change I found. Can you come pick me up?"

The girl obviously was too distraught to think rationally and too afraid to go back to her apartment. Kate couldn't let her down again. Never mind that it was after eleven o'clock, she saw when she checked her watch, or that Brady was sound asleep.

It's like nobody cares if I die in the street! the girl had shouted yesterday. Kate had replied that *she* cared. Now she meant to prove it. "Where are you exactly?"

Between sobs, Eve provided a street name and number. It was only a few miles away.

"I'll be there as soon as I can." Realizing Duane might be cruising around in search of his victim, Kate added, "Stay out of sight until you see me." She described her car.

"Okay. Okay."

After clicking off, Kate put on her shoes and went to lift Brady gently from bed. "We're going to rescue a friend," she told him. "You can doze in the car, all right?"

He mumbled and curled against her. Had he gained twenty pounds when she wasn't looking, or was that the effect of her pregnancy? Kate wondered as she carted him to her car and strapped him into the child seat.

Thank goodness she didn't have to worry about getting the ignition started tonight. She had more than enough other things to think about.

At this hour, the town loomed dark and deserted. She didn't see anyone on the side streets, and on Safe Harbor Boulevard, most of the shop were shuttered. Despite a scattering of streetlights and the occasional glare of an oncoming car, the town seemed sunk in gloom.

The convenience store was located near the freeway, surrounded by older apartment buildings. As she turned into the parking lot, Kate noted an elderly man leaving the store with a bottle-shaped paper bag under his arm, and a couple of tattooed guys lounging against a souped-up car.

What a foolish risk for a pregnant woman to come here with a little boy, she thought. If Eve weren't counting on her, she'd turn around and go home. Instead, she slowed and rolled around the side of the building, her tires crunching over discarded cans and plastic bottles.

Tony would advise her to call the cops, she supposed, and he'd be right. But she needed to calm Eve first. Panic and distress weren't good for her baby, and things would be even worse if the girl panicked and fled.

The thought of Tony stirred longing and regret. Kate had hated arguing with him. She hadn't intended to challenge him about Tara, only to share her feelings. Now he'd probably never trust her again. He'd certainly been quick to stand on his legal claims, though. Why couldn't he relax and hear her out?

A sudden movement set Kate's heart pounding. She

braked instinctively, and nearly panicked as someone tugged at the door handle. Then, through the window, she saw Eve's tear-streaked face.

The girl slid inside the instant Kate unlocked the door. "Thank you. I'm freezing." Eve wore only a short terry robe against the cool evening.

"Any sign of him?" Kate asked.

"I saw his pickup cruise by, but he didn't see me." Eve shrank as low as the seat belt would allow, presumably trying to become invisible. "I'm sure he wants revenge because I had him arrested. How could they let him out?"

"I don't know." Kate supposed judges who set bail in cases like this had to follow rules, but whoever set those rules ought to be the ones threatened, so they'd understand.

"Mommy? Who's this?" asked a drowsy voice from the rear seat.

"This is my friend Eve. Eve, this is Brady."

Her passenger peered back in surprise. "You brought your kid?"

"I couldn't leave him alone."

"Wow. I'm sorry you had to bring your little boy. Sorry, bud," she told Brady.

"It's okay," he muttered.

The girl pulled her robe tighter. "I didn't mean to yell at you yesterday," she told Kate.

"I'm sorry I reamed you out." As she drove, she kept an eye out for a truck, but apparently Duane was searching elsewhere. "Does he have a key to your apartment?"

"Yeah. If I hadn't heard him fumbling with the lock..." Eve shuddered. "The weird part is, I have to move out tomorrow anyway. One more day, and he'd have missed me."

"Where are you planning to go?"

"Haven't figured that out yet."

Maybe Samantha knew of a social service that could help. Or Tony… But Kate wasn't sure she dared involve him. It might be wise to keep their private lives separate from now on.

Wise. But lonely.

When they reached her house, she scooped up Brady and led the way inside. Relief radiated through her as she locked the door behind them.

Once she'd put her son to bed, she fixed two cups of herbal tea and, with Eve's permission, relayed the facts to the police. The dispatcher promised to send officers to take a report and put out an APB on Duane.

A few minutes later, two uniformed officers, a man and a woman, arrived. The woman introduced herself as Officer Hartman and the man as Officer Franco.

Kate gave a start at the name. "You must be Tony's brother."

"Yes, I'm Leo. How do you know Tony?" Although his light brown hair was cut shorter, it had the same defiant cowlicks, Kate noted.

"He's…um…" Now, this was tough to explain, she mused as her hand strayed to her bulge.

He made the leap immediately. "You're the surrogate."

"That's me," she admitted.

"Surrogate, huh?" asked his partner. "You're carrying this guy's nephew?"

"Niece," Kate said. "And, yes."

"Cool."

Officer Hartman took Eve's statement while Leo accompanied Kate into the kitchen to talk privately. His features reminded her so much of Tony's that she felt instantly comfortable with him.

After she finished providing her account of the night's events, he said, "You drove out in the middle of the night to help that girl?"

"I couldn't let her down."

He arched an eyebrow. "You're certainly nothing like Esther." His tone made it clear he wasn't fond of his sister-in-law.

"She seemed nice when we were arranging the surrogacy," Kate said cautiously. "I hope she and Tony can work this out."

"Work what out?"

He didn't know about the divorce? "I don't think I should talk about it."

"She bailed on him?" Leo gave a mirthless laugh. "Doesn't surprise me. She's a barracuda. But hey, they suit each other."

Before she could decide on a response, his partner joined them. "Miss Benedict's awfully shook up. I can call around to the women's shelters, but frankly, she'd be better off with friends."

"She can stay here tonight, Officer Hartman." To Kate, that seemed obvious.

"You sure the perp doesn't know your address?" the woman asked. "And call me Patty."

"Thanks. No, he doesn't."

Eve peered in from the living room. "I can stay tonight? Really?"

"You bet."

After the officers left, Kate insisted that Eve sleep in her bedroom, and found her an extra toothbrush. "People at work gave me more second-hand maternity clothes than I can wear. Tomorrow, we'll find a clean outfit for you."

"I can't tell you how much this means." The girl hugged her. They both ended up giggling because of the way they had to adjust their stomachs. "You sure you're okay on the couch? I didn't mean to take your bed."

"The couch will be fine."

Kate didn't entirely mean that; she expected to shift around uncomfortably for a while. Yet it seemed that no sooner had she changed into her nightgown and lain down beneath a cover than she was waking up to bright sunlight.

At first she felt wonderfully rested. Then a jolt of anxiety ran through her. How could she have forgotten to set an alarm? Brady would be late for school.

"Oops! I spilled some." His words drifted from the kitchen.

"It's okay...not much," replied a soft voice she recognized as Eve's.

Memories from last night flooded in. The drive in the dark. Her visitor. And of course the fact that this was Saturday.

After folding and putting the sheets away, Kate wandered in to see what the pair were doing. Baking brownies, she discovered, from a box of mix that she'd left on the counter along with a baking pan and mixing bowl.

"You were going to make these today, right?" Eve, still in her robe, was helping Brady spread gooey chocolate in the glass pan.

"Yes. What fun's a weekend without chocolate?" At the table, a couple of cereal boxes awaited, along with a bowl and spoon clearly set out for her. "You're kind to do all this."

"Are you kidding? Brady's my buddy!"

"Wanna play with my Transformers?" the little boy asked.

"Let's put this in the oven first." A moment later, the pair scampered away, as if they were both kids.

After breakfast and a shower, Kate helped Eve select a pale pink maternity top and dark pink jeans that suited her coloring. While Brady watched his favorite cartoon, Kate trimmed the younger woman's scraggly hair into a flattering style.

The process reminded her of the makeovers she'd arranged on Thursday. Kate had been delighted to see the girls on the news that same night: first old footage of their protest, followed by a busy scene at the beauty shop. True to her word, Jennifer had made clear that this was a special event, courtesy of My Fair Lady salon.

"Did I tell you I used to be in foster care?" Eve's comment snapped Kate back to the present.

"No. When?" She took a final snip at the bangs.

"I was fourteen." Eve's nose wrinkled beneath a shower of cut hairs.

"Where was your mom?"

"Doing six months in jail for drunk driving." Just as Kate was wondering why she'd brought this up, Eve added, "My foster mom, Hilda Warden...I mean, Warren...wanted to keep in touch after I left, but Mom said no. Do you think I'm too old for foster care? Just until the baby's born?"

"Once you turn eighteen, you're considered an adult." Still, the foster mother had offered continuing contact. "Couldn't hurt to call her, though. She might know someone who helps young mothers like you."

"I wish I could remember her phone number. It might be at the apartment."

"We'll have to arrange to collect your stuff." Kate brushed the stray hairs off Eve's face.

"Are you done?" the girl asked eagerly.

"You look great. See for yourself." As Kate produced a small mirror, the doorbell rang.

Eve froze. "What if it's Duane?"

"Stay out of sight. Get ready to dial 9-1-1." Despite a squeeze of fear, Kate hurried into the living room, only to spot Brady with his hand on the knob. "Wait!" How many times had she warned him never to open the door without her present?

"It's okay." He pulled it wide.

On the porch stood Tony. Overcome with relief, Kate swayed and caught the edge of the sofa for support.

He strode across the room and grabbed her shoulders, his worried face close to hers. "Are you okay? What's wrong?"

"I thought it was Duane. Eve's boyfriend." Embarrassed by her show of weakness, Kate straightened.

Gently, Tony released her. "Leo stopped by this morning and told me about your crazy rush to the rescue. Kate, you should have let the police handle it. Or called me."

"Eve needed my help."

"Yes, but…" He shook his head in frustration.

"She's fine, I'm fine and the baby's fine," she told him.

"You ran an unnecessary risk."

"Are you my keeper now?" she challenged.

"Certainly not. However…"

Eve peered into the room. "Oh! Good morning, Mr. Franco. What're you doing here?" Her gaze traveled between the two of them. "Whoa! Are you the surrogate dad?"

Tony ducked his head. "That's right."

"His wife went bye-bye," Brady piped up, and lifted a framed photo from the table. "She was here but now there's a teddy bear."

"Cute." Eve swung around as the timer rang. "Anyone for brownies?"

"Me!" Brady shrieked.

Grateful for the icebreaker, Kate said, "Me, too."

"I'll have a few." Obviously realizing no one would listen to anything he had to say, Tony accompanied them to the feast.

But this was, Kate suspected, only a temporary break at best.

Chapter Ten

On the plus side: delicious brownies. The fun of watching Brady stuff his little face while Kate laughed at his messy cheeks. The chance to help Eve by accompanying her to the apartment.

On the not-so-fun side: watching for any sign of a lurking ex. Lugging out Eve's TV set, computer and suitcases while she gabbed on her cell with her former foster mother, catching up on every detail of the past five years.

Most frustrating: letting Kate and Eve make all the arrangements instead of taking charge as he usually did. Not that their plans weren't reasonable, but Tony had never been relegated to the role of bodyguard-cum-driver before.

When they arrived at the ranch-style home of the foster mom, Hilda Warren, she scarcely acknowledged Tony's or Kate's presence as she threw her arms around Eve. "I'm thrilled that you called. Like I said, my husband died last year, and my daughter and her husband moved to Boston, so I'm rattling around in this place. It'll be wonderful to have you stay awhile," she chatted as they traipsed inside.

"How long a while?" Tony asked from behind.

"We'll figure that out as we go," Mrs. Warren assured him. "That's always worked for me."

He didn't relish seeing Eve out in the street again,

which might very well happen if she and her new hostess crossed swords. "You should agree on the house rules in advance," Tony warned. "Writing them down will prevent misunderstandings."

The graying woman regarded him with a twinkle. "I've helped raise more than a dozen foster kids, along with my daughter. Believe me, I'll have no trouble setting house rules."

He subsided. In court, once you'd raised your objection, you accepted the judge's decision with good grace.

"Where's my bedroom?" Eve rushed into the interior of the house, which to Tony smelled like laundry soap and cedar chips. "Oh, what adorable mice! I don't remember you having those."

"They're hamsters. When my great-aunt died last year, no one else in the family would take them, so I did."

"Can I see?" Brady begged.

"You bet." Hilda caught his hand and they hurried off together. The woman limped a little. Arthritis, Tony assumed.

Left alone with him in the living room, Kate said, "You've been a great help today, but you can lighten up. Hilda seems quite competent."

"Matters go more smoothly when people make their expectations clear," he explained.

Kate's teasing expression vanished. "I see."

She thought he was referring to the surrogacy agreement, Tony realized. Damn. He'd driven to her house today out of concern for her well-being, not a desire to revive their quarrel. "I'm speaking in general terms."

"Don't you ever forget you're a lawyer?" she challenged.

"I wasn't *born* an attorney," he said in surprise. "I

guess I do tend to view the world through the filter of my experience. Don't you?"

"I notice people's hairstyles, but I refrain from critiquing them," she replied.

"Mom!" came Brady's voice. "Come look!"

With an apologetic shrug, Kate obeyed, and Tony followed. He wasn't particularly interested in seeing the cage of small golden rodents with dark eyes and stumpy tails, though. He was too absorbed in trying to puzzle out how a man who'd won trophies in debate could keep losing arguments he hadn't knowingly entered.

Mostly, he wanted to mend fences without compromising his intention to raise his daughter alone. It made no sense for Kate and him to be at odds for the next five or six weeks until the birth. He wished she trusted him more, whether in the matter of midnight rescues or anything else.

People had *always* relied on Tony, from his mother and sister to his friends and his coworkers. Even Esther used to value him as her sounding board during most of their marriage.

"Don't stick your finger between the bars," Kate warned Brady. The little boy was reaching toward a hamster, which eyed Brady's finger as if it were a carrot.

"He likes me!" her son protested.

"For lunch, maybe," Tony said.

Brady giggled.

"You should get your little boy a pet, Kate," Eve said. "Animals give you unconditional love."

"Maybe someday. Right now, I've got my hands full."

"That's not the only thing that's full. Congratulations," Hilda said brightly. To Tony, she added, "You can bring in Eve's belongings. I'll show you her bedroom."

Obviously, these women were in no condition to cart

Eve's stuff in, so Tony ignored the ache in his shoulders from hauling everything out of her apartment earlier. Besides, to his amusement, Brady insisted on helping.

First the boy carried in a cosmetics bag, followed on the next trip by a pile of towels. "You're quite a helper," Tony said.

"We men have to stick together," the little guy responded.

Suddenly Tony didn't mind being ordered about by Mrs. Warren. "Darn right, bucko," he said.

"What's a bucko?"

"A tough guy."

"Yeah!" The kid high-fived him and dropped the towels.

Tony scooped them up and brushed off the dirt. "We don't have to tell anyone about this. A little dust never hurt anyone."

"Okay."

A long-forgotten memory came back, of being thirteen and unloading his parents' car at the beach house they'd rented on Balboa Island, a dozen miles from here. While their parents were inside, he'd told his ten-year-old brother which bags to take and how to avoid spilling the contents. Bossy, that's what Leo had called him.

When had they drifted so far apart? He hadn't even told Leo about the pending divorce, his brother had pointed out this morning. Over a cup of coffee, Tony had apologized and explained the circumstances.

"A baby on the way and all that witch can think about is the care and feeding of her ego," Leo had summed up with an edge of anger.

"What did Esther ever do to you?" She certainly hadn't objected to Leo's role as best man at their wedding. Yet, come to think of it, they'd rarely seen him after that.

"Oh, nothing," Leo had said. "Let me know when my niece arrives. I might spring for a present."

It had been on the tip of Tony's tongue to mention that he'd chosen the name *Tara*. For some reason, he hadn't. Their sister's death was still a painful subject for both of them.

Now, as he glanced down at Brady's earnest face, it struck him that having children gave you a second chance. You couldn't go back and recapture what you'd lost with a sibling or a parent, but you could do things right with your kid. And maybe, by giving that youngster the attention and approval you'd craved when you were small, you could parent yourself a bit in the process.

They finished stowing Eve's possessions in the house. "See you Thursday!" she called as the threesome departed.

"See you!" Kate replied.

As they drove away, Tony reflected on what a rarity this was, to have a whole Saturday free. And he couldn't think of anyone he'd rather spend it with than this pair. Also, they'd left matters between them far too unsettled. "Listen, can we talk?"

"You're already talking," Brady pointed out from behind them.

And there are big ears listening, too.

"This might not be the best time," said Kate, apparently thinking the same thing.

"I could use some daddy training, if Brady's willing," Tony improvised. "There's a park about a block from the hospital. Maybe you and I can find a few minutes to chat, as well. Then I'll treat you both to lunch."

"Yeah!" The boy pumped a fist. "Hot dogs, okay?"

Tony glanced at Kate. "With coleslaw, not fries," she conceded.

He took that as a yes.

Lots of other families had the same idea, Tony discovered when they arrived. The place bustled with little groups picnicking and enjoying the sunny autumn weather.

As soon as they got out of the car, Brady grabbed Tony's hand and tugged him toward the busy swings. "Push me."

"Is it all right with you?" he asked Kate.

"Sure. I haven't been able to do that since I became pregnant." She indicated a vacant bench. "I'll wait here."

At the swing set, the only free seat hung between two older boys around ten or eleven who kept veering their swings into the air at dangerous angles. "Let's try the slide instead," Tony proposed.

"I want to swing! You promised."

Since Tony's arrival, the older boys had settled into a steady glide. "Okay. Let's give it a whirl."

Brady scrambled into place. Keeping the seat aligned, Tony began pushing, providing more and more lift until the boy squealed with delight.

Abruptly, their neighbors pushed off hard. He had no idea whether they'd exchanged glances, caught a second wind or simply decided to test him, but higher and higher they went, as if determined to fling themselves into orbit.

One boy leaped off in mid-arc, leaving his empty seat to career wildly. Irked, Tony caught the chain and brought it to a safe landing. The kid trotted back and reclaimed his seat without a hint of apology.

The other fellow torqued his body until Tony feared a midair collision. Why did the city allow this sort of behavior? Any fool could see the liability.

Don't you ever forget you're a lawyer?

Okay, fine. But how else was he supposed to think?

Maybe like a dad.

As one of the swings twisted dangerously close, his patience snapped. "Stop, right now!" His sharp tone made the guilty rider flinch. "Slow that thing down and straighten it out, or you're off the swings." He turned to the boy's friend. "That goes double for you."

He half expected a smart-aleck demand to know who'd appointed him playground sheriff. Instead, the boys stopped. "It's baby stuff anyway," one sniffed, and off they rambled.

Two moms with preschoolers hurried to take their places. "Thanks," one of them said.

"I was afraid to put my little girl on here," added the other.

"Glad I could help." Tony's best reward, though, was the proud grin on Brady's face.

He kept the swing going for a few more minutes. Then, to his relief, the boy spotted a couple of buddies from kindergarten and demanded to hop down. His feet had barely touched earth before he shot off to join them.

Tony sat beside Kate, who'd ditched her shoes and stretched her legs along the bench. He slid beneath them and plopped her knees over his lap. What a lovely, casually intimate way to sit, with her legs draped over him.

"I'm envious," she said.

"You mean because I got to push Brady?" he hazarded.

"Because dads have such booming voices. I'd have had to shout myself hoarse at those boys."

"I never thought about it that way." He'd heard of women attorneys who trained their voices into a lower register to ring with more authority. "We tend to take our own advantages for granted."

"When I figure out my advantages, I'll let you know."

"You're lousy with advantages," he said.

"Name three."

"Beauty, brains and chutzpah." The words came easily.

"Chutzpah, anyway." Kate's head turned as she checked on Brady. She did that every few minutes, he noticed.

He hoped he'd develop the same constant awareness of Tara's actions when he was talking to people. Multitasking. Now there was an advantage women had that he'd forgotten to mention.

The park was filled mostly with couples and moms and grandparents, but he spotted a few fathers who appeared to be flying solo. Divorced, perhaps, with weekend visitation. One young father ran about with his son, who must have been at least nine and grew increasingly squirmy as his dad insisted on throwing a ball with a group of kids. The boy's body language shouted, "Back off!"

By contrast, a paunchy fellow sat on a blanket on the grass, fervently punching buttons on a handheld device while his toddler waddled full speed toward a passing dog. Tony was debating whether to run interference when the dog's owner tightened his grip on the leash, squatted and showed the child how to approach an animal gently.

The men weren't all clueless. A fellow about Tony's age tussled playfully with a toddler while keeping watch over a school-age girl jumping rope with friends. Obviously, he multitasked just fine.

The girl stopped jumping. "Dad!" she called. "Aren't we supposed to pick up lunch for Mom? We'll be late."

The guy checked his watch. "That's right! Thanks for reminding me."

Okay, so he didn't have it down perfect. If that were Tony, he'd have set his cell-phone alarm. Problem solved.

Kate shifted, and he saw her bulge rippling. Tara must

be on the move. How fascinating to think of her inside Kate's body, nourished and protected, yet independent too.

As if in response, Kate hoisted herself to a sitting position and swung her legs around. "Everything okay?" Tony asked.

"My muscles are cramping. Besides, you wanted to talk, right?" She nodded toward Brady, who, with a borrowed toy shovel, was avidly digging in a sandy area alongside another boy. Halfway to China by now, no doubt. "This may be the only chance we get."

Tony had almost forgotten that request. Now he sorted out his thoughts quickly. "First, I have to make sure we agree about what happens after Tara's born."

Her jaw tightened. "We already discussed that."

"And?"

"I understand what I signed." With strained patience, she added, "I'm not trying to challenge you, Tony."

"Good. Because until the baby's born, I'd like us to get along. That's point number two, in case you're counting."

"We *are* getting along," she growled.

He decided against citing her unfriendly tone. "I plan to continue as your birth partner, if that's all right."

"It might help if you showed up for lessons." She winced. "Sorry for the sarcasm. Yes, I'd like you to continue."

"I must have a rare gift," Tony said ruefully.

"What do you mean?"

"You're the sweetest-tempered person I've ever met, and I make even you cranky."

"Me? Sweet-tempered?" She shot him a wry smile.

"Admit it. I try your temper."

"You can be frustrating at times, but what guy isn't?"

she replied. "I don't expect perfection, and I sure hope nobody expects it from me."

On the walkway, a young couple pushed a stroller past them. Across a swath of grass, an elderly man and woman walked hand in hand.

"I keep trying to figure out where I went wrong with Esther," Tony admitted. "I always believed marriages should last, if you're both reasonable people. I know my friends blame her for everything, and she *is* the one who left, but I can't be totally innocent, either."

She didn't rush to defend him. But then, he shouldn't have expected that. "Well, we each pick the person we marry. Chemistry's part of it, but there has to be more. Quinn was a daredevil. Looking back, I guess I craved vicarious excitement because I'm such a homebody. Then after we had a child, I expected him to turn into a family man."

"Did he?" Although Tony wasn't sure why, he cared about the answer more than he should have.

"He was getting there. What about Esther? What drew you to her?"

He visualized her at the alumni gathering where they'd run into each other again after law school. Tall, intense and magnetic, she'd turned heads as she moved from group to group. He'd felt pleased when she recognized him and her face lit up with welcome.

"She was exciting and dynamic," Tony conceded. "We shared a lot of interests and tastes. She's more outgoing than I am, too. I get along with people but I don't tend to form close friendships."

"Who's your best friend?"

He'd never thought about it. "Mark, I suppose."

"Dr. Rayburn?" Kate sounded dubious. "You hang out together?"

"We play golf occasionally."

"Who do you talk to when you have a problem?" she asked.

You. The instinctive response surprised him. "I solve my own problems." Except he wasn't sure how he would solve the one that had just presented itself.

Sure, he'd drawn the line about raising Tara, Tony mused. The trouble was, when he drew it, he'd left his friend Kate on the other side. Who was he going to open up to once she disappeared from his life?

Brady pelted up. "I'm hungry!"

"Hot dogs, as promised." Catching Kate's hand, Tony gave her a boost, and kept a light grip as they set out across the park. With so many kids racing about, he wasn't willing to risk her being jostled.

To everyone else, they must look like a happy couple with a delightful son and another child on the way. And, for a moment, they almost were.

Chapter Eleven

"She's too strict. I don't mind feeding the hamsters, and she does clean their cages, but she watches everything I eat. I missed my vitamins one morning and she was all over my case." Eve paced around the clinic's front room.

A used desk and an almost-new couch had replaced the folding chairs. Cash donations generated by the television publicity had gone into a fund to hire professional staff. But as of this Thursday, Kate remained the only counselor and Eve the only client.

"She's treating you like a child," Kate summarized.

"Yeah! She forgets I'm not fourteen anymore." Now that her bruise had healed, and with her hair fluffed attractively, Eve appeared less like a victim and more like a confident young woman.

"You're still working part-time?"

"That's another thing. Hilda says it's bad for me to be on my feet waiting on customers, but my boss is talking about giving me more hours. Maybe even putting me on full-time. Then I'd have benefits."

Tony had had the right idea when he suggested the pair put their rules into writing. Still, this conflict went beyond mere regulations. "Want my advice?"

Eve paused by the window, soft morning light playing

over her fair skin. "That's why I'm here. No more storming out in a snit, I promise."

"Hilda's used to being a mother hen to her little chicks. In order for her to change, you've got to inspire her to see you differently." To head off objections, Kate hurried on. "Start acting like an equal."

"That's what I keep telling her!"

"Don't tell her. Mother her."

That gave the young woman pause. "What do you mean?"

"Spend some of your money on things for the household, for both of you. Also, she has arthritis, correct?" Receiving a nod, Kate continued, "Take the burden off her without being asked. Do chores. Fix her tea. Scold her—nicely— when she pushes herself too hard."

"She needs to see a doctor about the arthritis instead of toughing it out," Eve said. "I'll nag till she makes an appointment. How's that?"

"Excellent start."

"She's down in the dumps about the holidays, too. When her husband and daughter were around, Thanksgiving used to be her favorite holiday. I don't suppose I'll be much of a substitute."

Since Kate was hosting her family's celebration this year, why not invite them? "That gives me an idea. Why don't you and Hilda—"

A tap at the open doorway cut her off. For a confused instant, she wondered why Tony was wearing a uniform, and then she registered that this was his brother. "Leo. Hello! What brings you here?"

"Somebody isn't picking up her phone messages." The officer indicated Eve. "Took a little digging, but I tracked her down, thanks to her new landlady."

Eve scowled. "I haven't done anything wrong."

He folded his arms. "I wanted to give you the news. We arrested your friend Duane last night for holding up a gas station."

"Sounds like him, the jerk!"

"Was anybody hurt?" Kate asked.

"No, but he had a gun, and he's got a couple of priors," Leo said. "The judge won't set bail this time."

Eve appeared torn between relief and dismay. "I'm glad he can't bother me again, but I hoped he'd straighten out and help support us."

"I suspect the state of California will be supporting *him* for a few years," Leo remarked.

"It was kind of you to bring Eve the news in person," Kate put in.

"No big deal. I was coming to the hospital to visit a friend anyway."

"Yeah, thanks." Eve seemed to realize she'd been ungracious.

"Will she have to testify against him?" Kate hated to see Eve put through that stress.

"It's up to the district attorney. But maybe not. We've got plenty of evidence to nail him for the armed robbery."

"That's good," Eve conceded. "Sorry about not picking up my messages."

"Is this friend you're visiting a fellow officer?" Kate put in. "I hadn't heard of anyone being hurt on duty. You guys do such a great job of protecting us." Safe Harbor's force had an excellent reputation.

"No. She's a dispatcher. Just had a baby." He indicated Kate's bulge. "How's my niece?"

"Healthy and kicking. Emphasis on the kicking." How strange to think that, in the future, this man would have a closer connection to Tara than Kate would. She refused to dwell on how much that prospect hurt.

"Glad to hear it."

Impulsively, she said, "I was about to invite Eve and Hilda to Thanksgiving dinner at my house. We'd be delighted for you to join us if you aren't working." After all, Leo had gone out of his way to be helpful today, and he *was* Tara's uncle.

"I'll be on night shift," he said. "So I'm free earlier. But…"

"You're inviting us?" Eve put in. "I'd love it. I won't let Hilda say no."

"The more the merrier."

"That's kind of you." Leo hesitated. "Not sure I should, though."

"Sausage-and-raisin stuffing," Kate murmured. "Pumpkin pie, although I'll probably cheat and buy those."

"Baked yams?" he asked.

"Absolutely. Your favorite?"

A nod. "Once we got older, our parents had the meal catered. Never seemed right to me. Not that I object to your buying the pies. In fact, I'd like to bring those. How about a pumpkin, a pecan and an apple?"

"That would be fabulous. I'm not sure how many people are coming." Kate conducted a quick mental count. "Nine or ten, maybe a dozen." Her mom might want to include a friend or two from the senior center.

"Maybe I should make it four pies, then," he deadpanned.

"Did somebody mention pie?"

As Tony joined them, Kate gave herself a mental poke. Why hadn't she considered that he would find out about his brother coming to her place for Thanksgiving? Still, he'd already turned down her invitation to join her family for the holiday. And that might be for the best.

The closer they got, the harder it would be to untangle

their lives after the birth. Last night in class, when they'd practiced relaxation exercises, his soothing words had instructed Kate to tense and then release each group of muscles. Instead of relaxing her, though, his low voice had produced shivers of excitement. As if that weren't bad enough, Tina had encouraged the partners to stroke the part of the woman's body that was supposed to relax. Her arm. Her shoulder. Her stomach. Afraid her reaction might become apparent, Kate had pleaded a full bladder and fled.

She realized Tony was studying her expectantly. "Thanksgiving," she explained. "You turned me down, remember?"

He regarded her uncertainly. "You're inviting all these people to your sister's?"

"I'm cooking this year."

"It's at your house, Kate? I rescind my no vote."

She couldn't very well object. "That's great."

"We'll bring stuff, too," Eve insisted. "Like, a couple of Hilda's favorite recipes. Okay if I let you know the details next week?"

"That'll be fine." Silently, she noted how much more adult Eve sounded already.

They spent a few more minutes discussing the merits of baked versus deep-fried turkeys—a fire hazard, in Leo's opinion—and whole-berry versus regular cranberry sauce, then Eve and Leo departed. Alone with Tony, Kate stared down at her hands, suddenly unsure what to say.

"I'm taking a lot for granted, aren't I?" Tony asked.

"I did invite you."

"Circumstances have changed since then," he conceded. "I won't come if you'd rather I didn't."

His controlled tone failed to hide a note of pain. Looking up, she saw the sadness in his eyes. "I'd love to have you there. It's just…well, I was afraid you'd feel uncomfortable."

"Because I'll never see any of those people again? Except Leo," he added. "That doesn't mean I have to avoid them now."

"I thought we were trying to keep our lives separate."

His arm encircled her. "That was a couple of conversations ago. I thought the latest was that we're staying friends until the baby's born." His lips traced her temple.

She rested her cheek against his shoulder, relishing the smooth weave of his jacket, the fragrance of his aftershave lotion. If he kissed her, she might melt. Or cry. Or grab him by the tie and do utterly inappropriate things, considering that she was eight months pregnant and he was still married.

The room echoed with their rapid breathing. Kate wished someone would barge in. Samantha, or Dr. Rayburn, perhaps.

No one did.

"How many people?" Tony asked.

How many people what? Oh. "Eight. Ten. The number keeps growing."

"Let's have it at my place."

That woke her up. Kate took a step back. "You're kidding."

"Why not?" he demanded. "It's bigger, and our—my—kitchen's a work of art. I've got wedding gifts we never used, in spite of the fact that we bought the house with entertaining in mind."

"But those are Esther's gifts," she protested.

"She told me to keep the kitchen stuff, except for a few essentials. Cooking isn't her thing."

Too many logistical problems. "Cooking for Thanksgiving isn't a matter of a few hours. I have to start shopping days in advance. Fix some of the dishes ahead. Set up the table and get out the china."

"All the more reason to put me to work." Tony cupped his hands around hers. "Kate, I need to learn this stuff. How to plan and organize and cook. How to be part of a family. By the way, I'm paying for the food."

She stiffened. "This is *my* dinner."

"It's everyone's. They're all bringing food, right? Best of all, I can have my cleaning service polish off the mess the next day." He kept her hands cradled between his. "You get to take as many leftovers as you want, I promise."

No squeezing around a too-small table, eating off paper plates. No worries about whether she could afford all that food. She was weakening. But how could she justify having the event at Tony's, especially to her sister? Grasping at straws, Kate blurted, "Isn't Lori and Jared's wedding reception just a week or so later? They'll probably want to start setting up in advance."

"You didn't hear?"

"Hear what?"

"They've postponed the wedding indefinitely."

That stunned her. Lori had seemed so happy. "Why on earth? This isn't because her matron of honor ran out on her, is it?"

"No, that's one thing Esther *didn't* manage to wreck." He shook his head. "Jared's discovered he's hungry to be a father. And Lori's dead set on never changing another diaper."

Even though Kate couldn't imagine not wanting children, her heart went out to the bride-not-to-be. "She thought they were perfect for each other."

"So did he. At least they discovered their incompatibility before the wedding." Tony's thumb traced each of Kate's fingers in turn, massaging them lightly. "The other day, I never finished answering your question about why I married Esther. We dovetailed in so many ways that I took it for granted we'd adapt naturally as our lives progressed."

"Only you didn't?"

The massage shifted to the backs of her hands, which, like her fingers, had become puffy during the pregnancy. "To me, everything appeared to be moving along the right track. When we learned she couldn't conceive, we found you. That suited me fine, but I think deep inside her, a switch got flipped."

"No more mommy hormones, on to the next target?" Kate summed up.

"Esther's a bulldog about achieving success in whatever she aims for, and I suspect her subconscious found a new goal." His jaw worked. "Not that I'm excusing her. Casting us off in her personal pursuit of happiness is a rotten way to treat me, and you, and the baby."

More and more, Kate disliked hearing about Esther. She hadn't deserved a husband like Tony. *But that's none of my business.*

"About Thanksgiving. Before I tell everyone it's at your place, maybe we should give this more thought."

"Why don't you and Brady meet me at the house on Saturday afternoon?" Tony countered. "You can assess the kitchen, and if the weather's warm enough, I'll bet he'll enjoy a swim. That pool isn't used nearly enough."

It couldn't hurt to spend one afternoon there, could it? She had to admit, she was curious to dig through Esther's cabinets and see what fabulous gifts lay there unused. "That'll be fun. But I'm not promising anything."

"No one said you were."

She'd yielded more than she meant to. On the other hand, two bathrooms downstairs and an uncounted number upstairs. A game room to keep the kids out from underfoot. A housekeeping crew to clean up.

This was going to be hard to resist.

Chapter Twelve

After a family dinner at Mary Beth's on Friday, Kate explained the latest developments to her sister and mother. "I haven't said yes, but Tony has a beautiful house. Far more comfortable than mine."

"I'm dying to see it." Irene's needles clicked as she knitted a green rectangle.

The three of them had Mary Beth's living room to themselves. Ray was working again, while their ten-year-old son, Ray Junior, and eight-year-old, Johnnie, were entertaining Brady with their toys.

Kate had insisted on bringing dinner—roast chicken, mashed potatoes and salad—rather than impose on her sister. Nevertheless, judging by the frown lines on Mary Beth's forehead, her mood was anything but mellow.

Sure enough, her next words were, "That man thinks he can buy anything. He can't buy our family *or* our holiday."

Although taken aback by her sister's angry response, Kate refused to dismiss Tony's offer that easily. "His house-cleaning service will handle the cleanup the next day. All we'll have to do is clear the table and rinse a few things. There'll be plenty of bathrooms, and we can take leftovers home."

"Bathrooms are good." Irene cast a wary glance at her elder daughter. "Don't you agree?"

Mary Beth scowled. "As if the pilgrims worried about things like that!"

"You aren't usually like this. What's the matter?" Kate caught her breath, wondering if she'd stepped into a minefield. Lori and Jared's postponement of their wedding and Tony's breakup with Esther reminded her of the fragility of relationships. What if Ray's absences reflected more than simply a busy schedule?

"Nothing."

The click of the knitting needles and boyish chatter from down the hall punctuated the silence that followed. Distressed, Kate wondered how to continue without further infuriating her touchy sister.

The green rectangle grew longer. "What're you knitting?" she asked absently. "It almost looks like a... Mom, is that a baby blanket? You guys aren't expecting me to keep Tara, are you?"

"After you've told us endlessly about your precious contract?" Mary Beth snapped. "Certainly not."

"Tell her." With that cryptic remark, Irene gathered her knitting and stood. "I'm going to check on the kids."

"They don't need checking." Mary Beth broke off as their mother left the room.

"When did you stop talking to me?" Kate asked. "I love you. What's wrong?"

Tears filled her sister's eyes. "I'm pregnant."

What was wrong with that? At thirty-two, Mary Beth remained young enough for another child, and both her previous pregnancies had gone smoothly. Perhaps she'd have the girl she longed for, although she and Ray would be happy with another boy, Kate knew. "That's wonderful."

"I thought you'd feel awful!" her sister exclaimed. "I

mean, I'm glad, even though the pregnancy wasn't planned. But my baby will be close in age to yours. Every time you look at him or her, you'll be reminded of Tara. How could I possibly celebrate a holiday with that man, knowing what he's taking away from you?"

"She's Tony's daughter, too," Kate admonished. "I'm sorry you've been distressed when you ought to be overjoyed."

"You'll be devastated. Don't tell me you won't! This whole business was a bad idea, but as long as he had a wife in the picture, I understood his position. Now he ought to let you keep Tara. Honestly, how is he going to raise a baby?" Her voice quavered.

Kate moved across the room to hug her sister. "I'm thrilled for you and Ray. I was afraid maybe you guys were having problems."

"Us?" Mary Beth wiped away a tear.

"The way you've been acting. And he's never here."

"We're fine." She gave Kate a shaky smile. "I've been worrying about *your* reaction."

"I won't pretend giving up my daughter will be easy," she admitted. "But I can't blame Tony."

"He treats you like some sort of peasant!"

"You've never met him."

"And I don't plan to. Especially not on Thanksgiving. Please say you're not having the dinner there. I can't eat under his roof."

Kate hated having to make this choice. But she hadn't actually said yes to Tony. "I promised to check out his kitchen tomorrow. Brady's excited about swimming in the pool. But…" She inhaled deeply. "This is as much your celebration as mine. Okay. I'll explain that we can't accept his offer. But he's still invited to join us."

"I'll ignore him."

"Even if you're both waiting in line for the potty?"

"I'll hold it," her sister said.

They tapped their foreheads together, the way they used to when they were kids. A secret signal of accord.

"Now tell me all about this pregnancy," Kate demanded. "When did you find out? What's your due date?"

"Well, I'd been feeling sick to my stomach, so a few weeks ago…"

As her sister talked, Kate treasured their restored closeness. And tried not to worry about how to break the news to Tony tomorrow.

TONY LAID OUT a stack of towels by the pool and took another swing through the house. He'd like to be prepared to show Kate its many advantages. Although he wasn't sure why it mattered so much, he hoped she'd let him play host.

He supposed his behavior might seem inconsistent. He *had* declined her initial invitation weeks ago. But that was before he learned Leo was coming, before the location got switched away from her sister's home and before he'd realized that she'd become his best friend.

He'd never shared as much with anyone as with Kate. Talking to her opened up a sensitive place deep inside, casting light into the shadows. Before this, he hadn't even been willing to admit he *had* shadows.

He'd like for them to remain friends, but the potential legal complications of bending the surrogacy agreement would be devastating. This was his daughter, perhaps the only child he'd ever have.

What he ought to be thinking, Tony supposed, was, *If only my wife hadn't left.* He really should be regretting that more. Or, on the other hand, feeling angry and betrayed, the way he had initially. Instead he felt as if losing Esther wasn't such a bad thing after all.

At least for once he would enjoy a home-cooked meal for Thanksgiving, instead of a coldly perfect catered meal at her parents' house. Why was it that professional chefs, brilliant on every other occasion, somehow missed the spice that made this holiday meal special?

Perhaps because that spice was love.

He walked through the ground floor, trying to see it as their guests might on the holiday. In the two-story entryway bathed in sunshine from the overhead skylight, a staircase curved upwards. To the left lay the dining room, with the living room to the right. He followed the hall back into the family room with its giant TV and array of video equipment, and glanced into the state-of-the-art workout room Esther had installed to save driving to a gym.

Impressive. But hardly vibrating with warm memories. So far, anyway.

Tony retraced his steps, then headed through the breakfast room to the kitchen. Beyond it lay the bay-windowed sunroom. Not an item out of place, not a fingerprint on the walls.

When he and Esther bought the house three years ago, they'd planned to entertain here. And they had, on exactly three occasions. They'd held a housewarming for friends and colleagues, a birthday bash when his wife turned thirty, and a party for her parents' fortieth anniversary.

That had been a formal affair, with waiters serving cocktails and the guests wearing tuxedos and designer gowns. In addition to raking in millions as a builder, Esther's father had served on the Orange County Board of Supervisors. He'd once run for the state legislature, but lost in the primary to a more colorful rival. The disappointment had scarred the man, and perhaps inspired his daughter's determination never to be second best at anything.

The opening notes of a Beethoven piano piece chimed from the front entrance. Tony glanced at the kitchen counter, where he'd arranged a tray of bakery cookies. They tasted as good as homemade; he knew because he'd eaten a couple. But they didn't make the house *smell* wonderful.

He strode to the door.

"Hi." Kate beamed at him, blissfully unaware of a dirt smear on her cheek. Her red-and-white checked maternity top floated merrily about her, while Brady stood beside her, a patch of sand stuck to his forehead. "Sorry for the mess. We went to the beach."

"Without me?" he asked, half joking and half, well, envious.

"It was a birthday party." As she followed him inside, Tony noted that Brady carried a backpack. Great way to cart around toys. "I can't believe how many invitations he gets. Some of his friends must have birthdays three, four times a year."

"Really?" the boy chirped. "Can I?"

"Your mommy's kidding," Tony told him. "You went swimming already?"

"Oh, no," Kate said. "The ocean's too cold."

"My pool's heated." He wasn't sure where to suggest they start—swimming or inspecting the kitchen?

Brady saved him the trouble by tearing up the stairs, then sat on his rear and bump-bump-bumped down again. "Whee! This is fun."

"Settle down," Kate reproved. "We're indoors, not at the park."

The boy lost his momentum partway to the bottom. "Can I slide on the rail? I saw that in a cartoon."

"Absolutely not!"

"How about a lift instead?" Tony crouched below him. "Climb on my back."

"He's heavier than he looks," Kate warned.

"I can handle him." Tony used to do this with Tara. By age twelve he'd reached nearly adult size while, at six, she'd remained small. "Put your arms around my neck."

A weight plopped onto Tony's back. Brady lost his balance and shouted, "Uh-oh!" Two wiry arms briefly cut off Tony's air supply. Trying not to choke, he shifted until Brady's grip loosened.

This had been a lot easier twenty years ago.

Kate merely observed with a sharp eye. She didn't fuss, the way Tony's mother used to when she caught him carrying Tara.

Descending the stairs with the boy's wiggly weight on his back proved a challenge, but once they were on solid ground, all Tony had to do was watch out for head-bumpingly low doorways. And hold steady when Brady sighted the video system in the family room and scaled down Tony as if he were riding a fireman's pole.

"Agile as a monkey," Tony muttered, rubbing a spot on his hip that the boy's shoes had grazed.

"I had no idea he would do that." Kate blocked her son as he scrambled toward the game system. "Young man, we are not here to play with a boob tube."

"Don't call it that!" the boy protested.

"Only boobs play with screens when there are other things to do," she chided.

On Kate's previous visit, Tony recalled Esther whisking her upstairs to the future nursery with barely a glance at the rest of the premises. "Let me show you around," he offered, and drew them both to the workout room.

Kate examined a cycling machine. "Impressive. Of course, these days I can't even touch my toes."

Brady hopped onto the treadmill. "Make it go!"

"Maybe later, sport. You're a little young." Tony jotted a mental note to put a lock on the door once Tara started walking. Equipment like this could present a hazard. "Let's check out the kitchen. I've got a treat for you."

"Brownies?" Kate guessed.

"Not quite."

"Fudge?" Brady jumped off the treadmill.

"Cookies. With chocolate chips," he added. "Also some with macadamia nuts."

"Yeah!" The little boy zoomed past him like a heat-seeking missile.

"Guess he's figured out where the kitchen is." Tony escorted Kate through the rooms.

"This place is beautiful." She cleared her throat. "Listen, I appreciate your offer, but since we talked..."

He couldn't let her finish, not when her tone implied she was about to decline. Instead, rather ungraciously, Tony broke into a lope and called to Brady, "Let me get you a plate for those cookies."

What a heel he was, cutting her off with such a lame pretense. But once she saw the kitchen, surely she'd change her mind.

He found Brady munching away, one cookie in each fist. Whatever he'd eaten at the birthday party obviously hadn't filled him up.

"They're good, aren't they?" Tony ate one, too. "Fresh-baked this morning at the Cake Castle."

"How could you resist making them here?" A little out of breath, Kate heaved through the breakfast room. She indicated the large center island and overhead rack hung with copper pans. "This place is a caterer's dream."

"Two sets of sinks, ranges and dishwashers," Tony noted.

"Two dishwashers?"

"Overkill, I suppose, but handy for company." He pointed out the built-in refrigerator, trash compactor and other gadgets too numerous to count. All gleaming and, like the rest of the place, practically unused. "Begging to be put to use," he concluded.

"About that," Kate said. "I'm afraid we— Stop right there!"

He turned to see Brady smearing chocolate handprints across the wall that connected the kitchen to the sunroom. "No big deal. That does wash off, right?"

From her purse, she produced a pre-moistened towelette and swooped down on her son. "You're a walking disaster," she reproved. "You know better than this."

She didn't yell, though, or freeze the boy with disapproval. She simply wiped off his hands and face, then used another towelette to remove the wall prints.

"I promised him a swim," she told Tony. "Otherwise I'd whisk him out of here before he finishes wrecking the place."

"It could use a little wrecking." He meant that. Heck, maybe he should have saved those handprints to show Tara how to behave like a kid. Otherwise she might grow up as repressed as he had.

Wait a minute. Where had that idea come from?

"What's in there?" Brady pointed toward a small cabinet door beneath the built-in window seat.

"Storage." Tony had forgotten about it. "Empty, I believe."

The boy yanked it open and peered inside. "Cool! It's a cave!"

Kate cast Tony an apologetic look. "He's not usually this hyper. I hoped he would burn off his energy at the party, but all that cake and ice cream offset the running around. Plus, this house is a kid's fantasy."

It was? "To me, it seems…well, austere."

"Seriously? It's full of fun stuff."

He recalled Brady's reaction to the video equipment and the treadmill. They *were* fun—but apparently their charms paled beside the allure of unused storage space.

Tony squatted beside the window seat. Only Brady's sneakers and jean-clad rump were visible as he tunneled beneath it. "Finding anything?"

"No. It's great!" The little voice echoed.

"Could be spiderwebs." He doubted the cleaning crew had ever swept there.

"Spiders are more scared of us than we are of them," Kate responded calmly.

"You're pretty blasé, aren't you?"

"Quinn and I took him camping when he was three. I admit, I worried a little about mountain lions."

"Mountain lions?" He resolved not to let Tara anywhere near the wilderness till she was at least…thirty.

"Don't forget I married a daredevil. Brady can't help inheriting some of those genes." She dug into her son's discarded backpack. "How about some toys under there?"

"My cars." A tiny hand reached out, accepted a couple of miniature racing cars and disappeared.

"He can entertain himself for hours," she told Tony.

"Let's poke through the kitchen. I have no idea what's in those cabinets," he admitted.

"If they're as empty as the cave, you're in trouble." To Tony's relief, she accompanied him across the wooden flooring without further argument. Perhaps curiosity and the top-of-the-line kitchen facilities were dissolving her reservations.

They opened the cabinets one after another, all neatly

arrayed with expensive china and crystal, pristine baking dishes, enough food processors and mixers and blenders to supply a restaurant, several high-tech coffeemakers and a cappuccino machine.

"Dazzling," Kate said wistfully. "Do you suppose there's a turkey baster? No, never mind. Listen…"

Tony knew he'd have to hear her objections at some point, but not yet. "What about decorations?"

"My mom usually makes a centerpiece with dried corn and gourds." She closed a cabinet with the air of a child emerging empty-handed from a toyshop. "My sister has a wreath we freshen every year. Nothing fancy."

"Who cares about fancy?" he said. "I'm planning a real Thanksgiving, not a set-piece from a magazine. Although this place could use some sprucing up."

"I appreciate your good intentions, but…" She caught his arm. "Quit fidgeting."

"Me?" He resisted the urge to duck from her grasp.

She released him, and smoothed out a wrinkle on his shirtsleeve. "I'm sorry. We have to hold it at my house."

"Why?"

Her mouth twisted. "I promised my sister. It's going to be a struggle for her just to be under the same roof with you, let alone under your roof. She's very upset about losing her niece."

"Losing her niece?"

"You and I aren't the only ones who're related to this baby," Kate said. "Mary Beth's watched the baby grow just like you have. Now she's pregnant too. The babies will be cousins, and they'll never meet. I agreed to the surrogacy, but she had no say in the matter."

He'd never thought about the impact on the rest of Kate's family of her giving up Tara. There was a grandmother in the picture, too, wasn't there?

Perhaps his first impulse in turning down her invitation had been correct, Tony supposed. He didn't belong with this family for the holiday. But did he have to be rational all the time? "Let me think about this for a few minutes. Maybe I can devise a brilliant strategy to win over your sister."

"I'm afraid that's impossible."

"But you'll listen?"

Kate shrugged.

She hadn't refused. "Let's go swimming. Brady's looking forward to it, right?"

To his relief, she acquiesced without further argument. "He is. And I'm sure he needs to wash off a few cobwebs."

That gave Tony an hour or so to devise a winning plan. And he would. When it came to hosting Thanksgiving dinner, failure was not an option.

Chapter Thirteen

Tony's house didn't merely have a pool. It had a waterfall that splashed between rocks and ferns into a curving, manmade pond suitable for swimming or cavorting, with an inset heated spa. On the far side, the view through a wrought-iron fence revealed the sun-dappled harbor far below, its waters skimmed by a flock of white sailboats.

While Tony and Brady swam, Kate lounged poolside. Of course, Tony didn't simply have a patio, either. The expansive deck served as a combination lounge and outdoor kitchen, with built-in grill and, to one side, a great stone fireplace. Abundant red-purple bougainvillea provided privacy from the neighbors.

What a lovely spot to celebrate Thanksgiving. Impossible, though. Kate had to put Mary Beth's happiness first.

Reclining in a chaise, she watched Tony dive porpoise-like beneath the water and emerge beneath Brady. The boy flung his arms around Tony and rose into the air shrieking with glee.

What a natural father Tony was turning out to be. Kate wished he could remain a part of their lives. But despite his presumably newfound tolerance for chocolate handprints, he hadn't transformed into the type of person to embrace the messy and unpredictable. He lived by rules. That was why he'd chosen the law as his field, and Kate respected that part of his nature just as she'd accepted her husband's risk-taking.

Yawning, Brady climbed out of the pool. Tony followed and swathed the boy in a towel. Evidently the day's activities had finally caught up, because within seconds Brady had curled up on a recliner and fallen asleep.

After drying off, Tony sat beside Kate. "Wish I could have a boy *and* a girl."

"I'm not volunteering again!"

He grinned. "You sure?" Then he caressed the checked top over her abdomen. Kate hoped he couldn't tell that her breasts tightened beneath the maternity bra. "What a gorgeous sight. Every day you look more like a…"

"Beached whale?"

His chuckle rumbled through her. "I was going to say fertility goddess."

Tara was moving again. Wonder animated Tony's face. "Does she do this a lot?"

"I'm so used to it, I hardly notice. It's going to feel strange, having just one person inside my body again."

He studied her intently. "I'm sorry I haven't been around more during the pregnancy. It's such a miracle, I hate having missed any part of it."

"Well, obviously, you had to miss the first part." Now, why had she blurted that? Kate could tell from his heightened color that he was picturing them making love…and so was she.

She did her best to release the image, but the warmth of his hand remained pressed to her abdomen. The day Tara was conceived, she'd lain on a cold examining table in the doctor's office, trying not to equate this clinical procedure with anything beyond a contractual arrangement.

What if Tony had been there—not in the doctor's office, but with her at home, conceiving a baby? He'd have kissed and stroked her, teasing her with his mouth and his body. She could feel him moving against her, and then deep inside her....

"What are you thinking?" he murmured.

The words sprang out before she could stop them. "I wish we'd made Tara the old-fashioned way."

He tensed, and removed his hand.

Kate's eyes flew wide open. "I don't know why I said that. Forgive me."

Tony blew out a sharp breath. "You and I are opposites, you know."

"Doesn't take a genius to figure that out," she answered. "But what do you mean, exactly?"

"When you think something, you share it," he explained. "I'm less open. A lot less."

"Holding everything inside must be exhausting."

"I'm trying to communicate more openly, now that I'm about to become a dad." He tilted his lounger to match the angle of hers, bringing them face-to-face. "You've helped tremendously with breaking down the walls, but it's hard. My family wasn't warm like yours. Not that I'm criticizing. They had to be strict to protect us."

"Why?"

"Because of our sister. I accused them of being overprotective, but I discovered the hard way that they were right." He shook his head. "Old business."

"Are you sure you don't want to talk about it?" Whatever he was referring to, it obviously still bothered him.

"I don't want the past to make me too rigid with Tara," he admitted. "Kate, it's important to me to celebrate the holiday here, this once. To change the way I feel about this house. Already, just having you and Brady here today, it feels more like a home."

"I wish I could say yes, but it isn't up to me."

"I need to fill my home with people other than colleagues and associates," he went on, talking as much to himself as to her. "People who never wear tuxedos except to weddings. People who bring their favorite dishes without worrying about whether they fit into some prearranged menu. Kids who see boring empty cabinets as caves."

She, too, loved the idea of entertaining everyone here. Still, she'd promised. "I can't disappoint my sister."

He smacked the chair arms. "I've got it!"

"What?"

"As soon as Brady wakes up, we'll drive over to your sister's and I'll present my case. If I can't persuade her, I'm a darn poor lawyer."

He had no idea what he'd be walking into. "Compared to my sister, the toughest judge you ever faced was a wimp."

"Please let me try."

For the two of them to meet before turkey day might ease the tension on the actual holiday, Kate supposed. Or it could backfire. "If you two fight, it'll wreck everything."

He considered for a beat. "If I see that I'm losing, I'll yield graciously."

"I suppose it's all right, then, if Mary Beth agrees."

Bristling with eagerness, Tony sprang to his feet and retrieved a yellow pad. Kate watched him rapidly fill the page with notes. Marshaling arguments tapped into a special part of him, she mused. He was in his natural zone.

But he was about to step into her sister's zone. Kate wouldn't want to take bets on the winner.

WHEN TONY WAS PREPARING to present his argument to Mary Beth Mulligan Ellroy—he'd learned his judge's full name, always a good idea—he'd imagined them sitting or standing face-to-face, focusing on the issue at hand. That had been his first mistake.

But not his last.

In the yard of the Ellroys' one-story home, two boys were weeding a flowerbed while a man in scruffy jeans pruned a large bush. As soon as they spotted their aunt and cousin, the boys dropped their spades and raced over.

"Hey, Brady!" called the younger one.

"Cool car," said his brother. "It's got computerized guidance, huh?"

"Sure does." As he helped Kate out, Tony acknowledged introductions, answered questions and tried to keep the names straight. Younger son, Johnnie, age eight. Older son, Junior, age ten. The dad, Ray, had a firm handshake and a sprinkling of gray in his brown hair.

"I understand you're taking daddy lessons," he told Tony affably. "Here's my contribution. You know how I got the boys to spend Saturday afternoon gardening? I promised them laser tag afterwards."

"Bribery. That works," Tony conceded. "Not a good tactic in the legal world, but I guess families are different."

"Oh, hey, that's merely the beginning," Ray said. "Wish I could join you for Thanksgiving this year. I've got lots more tips. On the other hand, I'm staying out of this whole where-to-hold-the-dinner discussion. Which reminds me, I haven't told Mary Beth about the laser tag outing yet."

"What laser tag outing?" demanded an irritable female voice.

Everyone turned toward the woman who'd rounded the corner of the house. Taller and more angular than Kate, she folded her arms as she awaited a response.

"Honey, this is Tony Franco," Ray said.

"I'll get to him in a minute." Mary Beth ignored Tony's

attempt to catch her eye and exchange polite greetings. "I was going to fix chicken and potatoes for you to grill. If you leave now, you'll never get back in time."

"How about if I grill tomorrow?" Ray asked.

"You're working."

"Late shift. I'll cook lunch, right after church."

"I suppose we can have pizza tonight. But check with me about this stuff next time!" Clearly, her mood bordered on truculent. Or maybe she'd crossed that border already.

"Mary Beth," Kate began, but halted as the front door opened to reveal a silver-haired woman.

She favored Tony with a smile. "I'm Irene."

"Tony Franco." They shook hands. "You must be Kate's mother." As if there could be any doubt, given the strong family resemblance.

"Tara's *grandmother*," Mary Beth emphasized tightly.

"I'm delighted to meet you," Irene said. "Come on in. You, too, you little rascal."

"Hi, Grandma!" Brady gave her a hug, and then dashed inside. His cousins, after putting their tools away and removing their dirty shoes, slammed in through the back door and accompanied him down a hallway amid gleeful joking and jostling.

Boys. Tony had to admit he'd have an easier time if Kate were carrying an Arthur instead of a Tara. But he could adjust.

Time to steer the conversation on topic, he decided when Mary Beth marched inside. "You have a lovely home. I gather you normally hold Thanksgiving dinner here." As he spoke, he glanced into the formal living and dining rooms. The crisp draperies, rumple-free couch and polished wood indicated these were reserved for special occasions.

"It's nowhere near as elegant as your house, I'm sure." Mary Beth led the adults through the family room, where toys filled a large bin and books overflowed shelves. She ran a home day-care center, Tony recalled.

"This isn't simply a matter of my having a bigger house," he said.

"Sure it is," she retorted. "You assume you can buy anything. Want a baby? Just write a check. Thanksgiving dinner? You've got more bathrooms than anybody else, so you win by default."

"Mary Beth!" Kate looked shocked.

Irene winced. "I'll let you folks work this out," she said, and took off down the hall. After casting a sympathetic glance at Tony, Ray did likewise.

In the kitchen, Mary Beth shoved a roll of aluminum foil into a drawer and thrust several spice containers into a cabinet. Apparently she'd taken them out for the chicken and potatoes.

"You're angry because I have more money than most people?" There went Tony's judiciously prepared case.

The woman spun to face him. Dark circles and deep frown lines around her eyes emphasized her anger. "There are some things no one should be able to buy. And—" she glanced apologetically at Kate "—that no one should sell."

"I'm not selling Tara!" Kate flared. "She'd never have been conceived, never have had a chance to be born without the Francos."

"If you're angry at me, fine," Tony said. "But leave your sister out of it."

Mary Beth formed fists, as if preparing for physical battle. "She isn't thinking straight. She's grieving for her husband, struggling to make ends meet, trying to raise her son alone. She was vulnerable and you took advantage, you and that— I don't want to pollute this house by saying what I think of your wife!"

"Where did all this come from?" Kate asked in astonishment.

To Tony, the answer was painfully obvious. "From the heart," he answered. Both women stared at him. "You love the baby, don't you, Mary Beth?"

"Of course! She's my niece."

"I love her, too," he said. "She's my daughter."

Her chest heaved a couple of times before she answered. "I'm not saying you ought to give up all rights. But Kate should be the one to raise her."

Tony reflected once again that, until today, he hadn't given much thought to the family that had loved Kate since childhood, that saw her practically every day. They'd helped pick up the pieces after her husband died and would be doing it again after she surrendered the baby.

Still, this wasn't their decision. "Unlike my wife, Kate's a woman who keeps her word, and you should respect that."

"I do." Mary Beth blinked blearily. "I apologize to my sister. But this is eating me alive."

Kate touched her shoulder. "You don't look well."

"I threw up twice this morning." Mary Beth brushed back a defiant lock of hair. "Guess my emotions are pretty close to the surface."

"I'm sorry if we hit you at a bad time," Tony said.

A shrug. "We need to get this over with. At least today I'm not surrounded by little kids."

"We'll never agree about the surrogacy," he conceded. "But this is a small town. We may run into each other, and when we do, I'd like us to be on pleasant terms. I'd also like to carry the memory of this one special holiday to share with my daughter when she's older."

Kate rinsed out a cloth and dabbed her sister's forehead. "It'll be more convenient for all of us to meet at Tony's.

Double ovens. Lots of bathrooms, as you mentioned. And two dishwashers."

"Two?" Mary Beth asked.

"There's a special beverage refrigerator, a regular fridge and a freezer," Kate added. "Plus an outdoor kitchen with a fireplace and a fantastic view. You should see for yourself."

"An outdoor fireplace? I've never seen one of those except in a magazine."

"The boys will love the heated swimming pool and spa. And the game system, if we let them use it," Kate noted. "How'm I doing? Do we have a sale?"

"Also, if it helps, I promise not to act like a rich jerk," Tony put in.

Mary Beth's shoulders shook. For a moment, he feared he'd reduced her to tears. Then she burst out laughing. "That's exactly what I expected from you!"

"Happy to disappoint," he said.

Kate's appreciative glance touched him. Regardless of the ultimate decision about where to host the dinner, he felt good about this meeting.

Mary Beth leaned against the counter. "I don't suppose it matters where we get together. It's going to be the same group of people whether we're at Kate's cottage or your palace. I have to admit, my mad dashes to the bathroom will be a lot easier if I don't have to wait in line."

"I hope you'll feel better by then," Tony told her.

The woman studied him wryly. "If we'd met under other circumstances, I might like you."

"I take that as a high compliment."

"Did I mention his brother's bringing pies?" Kate asked.

"What about the rest of his family?" Mary Beth inquired.

"Don't have any." He could see in her face that she was wondering about Tara's future. And so was he.

Maybe we should all gather every year. Then I wouldn't have to describe a family Thanksgiving to my daughter as if it were a scene from a fairy tale.

The notion shook Tony. He couldn't bend the rules that far. But how would he avoid these people for years to come? As he'd said, Safe Harbor was a small town. From the start, he'd figured that occasional glimpses of the surrogate could be handled discreetly, but Mary Beth's pregnancy raised the possibility of Tara attending school with her cousin.

Perhaps if he drew careful guidelines... Tony decided to postpone any further consideration of the matter until after the holiday. While he didn't expect the gathering to degenerate into a free-for-all like some dysfunctional families Leo had described, better safe than sorry.

Mary Beth asked a few more questions, but raised no further objections. After thanking her for changing her mind, Tony and Kate excused themselves, collected Brady and left.

"Wow. She actually folded," Kate murmured as they drove back to her house. "You were amazing."

"You're the one who sold her on the idea," he countered.

"What idea?" Brady asked from behind them.

"We're going to have Thanksgiving dinner at Tony's house," Kate explained.

"Wahoo!" he shouted. "Can I play in the cave?"

"You bet." To Kate, Tony said, "I'll notify Leo. Will you tell Eve?"

"Glad to."

For the rest of the ride, they discussed a schedule for shopping and cooking. Tony offered to hire a decorator to make the house festive, and was pleased that Kate acquiesced.

He tried not to worry about whether this would be the last time he ever saw most of these people. For now, he'd won his case.

He could hardly wait for the big day.

Chapter Fourteen

Kate wasn't sure exactly when she fell in love with Tony. It might have been while she watched him playing in the pool with Brady, his deep masculine laughter rumbling across the water as he swooped the boy into the air. Or perhaps when, instead of taking offense at Mary Beth's remarks, he treated her with respect and turned the joke on himself.

Most likely, she'd been falling in love with him for a long time, and denying it to herself. It was the craziest thing she'd ever done, short of the surrogacy arrangement.

How ironic that he was training to coach her through childbirth, to feed her ice chips and share her breathing as she gave life, and then walk away. With their daughter.

When she was younger, she used to live in the present. As the weeks passed, Kate devoutly wished she still had that knack. *Please let nothing change. Let us stay right here, in the middle of November, forever.*

Things did change, of course. At the hospital, more young women gave birth, and some relinquished babies. Several pregnant girls arrived at the clinic for counseling, and Samantha raised additional funds, although no official opening had been set.

Lori and Jared, unable to agree on having children, reluctantly called off their engagement. At Kate's checkups, the nurse's eyes appeared red-rimmed from crying.

On a cheerier note, Eve reported that she and Hilda were getting along much better and she'd been invited to stick around long-term.

"You wouldn't believe how badly she eats!" Eve confided during their last counseling session. "If I don't crack down, she buys chips and cupcakes. I have to watch her like a hawk."

"You really are mothering her," Kate observed with amusement.

"Well, she'd better shape up, because she's not feeding my baby that garbage. Did I tell you Hilda's going to be my birthing partner? Isn't that sweet?"

"It's like she's having a grandchild," Kate said.

"That's how I feel, too."

As for her own birthing coach, Tony arrived on time for the last three childbirth classes. Together they studied the second and third stages of labor, medications and complications. More importantly, he learned how to diaper, and what to do about the umbilical cord stump, and which symptoms in a newborn merited calling the doctor.

The baby noticeably gained weight. If Kate had felt enormous before, now she wished for a wheelbarrow to trundle her bulge around.

"It's worth it, though, isn't it?" Tina Torres enthused at the last class, and received a chorus of agreement.

Kate barely managed a smile. Because not only would she be giving up her daughter, she'd be losing Tony, as well. While it seemed inevitable that they'd run into each other, they'd be strangers. Worse than strangers, because there'd be no possibility of any further acquaintance.

One night she pounded her pillow and yelled—mentally, so as not to wake Brady—"Why can't you love me? What do I have to do, earn a law degree? How can you put your hands all over me in class and not feel this connection?"

At some level, he must. The day they went grocery shopping together, for instance, he made bad turkey puns until they nearly collapsed with laughter in the meat department at Ralph's. Another day when she was exhausted, he left her home and took Brady swimming at his pool, just the two of them. Brady was ecstatic, and Tony couldn't stop talking about what a great son she had.

But she knew which line never to cross: the issue of their surrogacy agreement. On that subject, he showed no sign of yielding. Ahead, the mid-December due date loomed like a block wall.

Kate preferred to concentrate on Thanksgiving. What a glorious diversion, with endless details to review with Tony. Should they serve outside, relying on heat lamps and the fireplace if the weather turned chilly? That might be fun, but common sense won out. Why risk a breeze blowing the linens around or sending some of Esther's good china crashing to the ground?

Finally, that special Thursday dawned. Kate got up early and drove to the clifftop home to stuff the turkey. While she worked, Tony and Brady conducted an earnest discussion of the merits of fresh yams versus canned, and pineapple versus marshmallow topping. Unable to narrow their choices, they checked out recipes on the Internet and made a last-minute trip to the supermarket to buy enough ingredients for *two* yam dishes.

Thank goodness for ample counter space and duplicate appliances, because, if they'd gotten in her way, Kate would have beaned them with the turkey baster she'd brought from home. Instead, their intent conversation and almost comical distress when they dropped things distracted her from the inconvenient positions dictated by her large abdomen.

With the turkey in the oven and the other dishes in good shape, she collected her yawning son for a nap. On the way out, she admired the decorator's work, which, in her eagerness to start cooking, she'd barely glanced at earlier. An elaborate cornucopia sprawled across a side table, sprays of rust-and-gold flowers highlighted the entry hall and, on the front door, cute stuffed-animal faces peered from a harvest garland.

The weather cooperated, too, sunny but brisk. En route home, Kate reflected that she couldn't have wished for a more perfect Thanksgiving.

Over an hour later, she awoke from her nap to feel her entire body tightening. An invisible hand seemed to clamp her bulge, squeezing until she felt like a tube of toothpaste.

No, no, no. Not today.

False labor, Kate assured herself. She'd felt a few random contractions before, although never this strong. Her body must be practicing for the big day. True, babies sometimes came a few weeks early, but Brady had been late, and so had her sister's two kids.

Feeling no further contractions, she relaxed after a while and put on a loose-weave dress with vertical stripes in autumn hues. Nothing could minimize her bulk, but she loved the festive colors.

Although the guests weren't scheduled to arrive until three, she and Brady returned at one for the countdown of final preparations. She consulted the chart she'd taped to a cabinet, and dug in.

"This is like a military operation," remarked Tony, busy peeling potatoes to boil and mash.

"That's for sure." Kate opened cans of cranberry sauce, transferred the contents into small bowls and put them in the fridge.

Twice more, her muscles squeezed, but the contractions weren't cutting closer together as with true labor. Still, they did feel strong.

While she was debating whether to mention them, Irene and Mary Beth put in an early appearance. Junior and Johnnie, who carried toy robots with flashing lights, raced to join Brady in his cave, which he'd discovered ran for quite a distance beneath the built-in window seat.

"We couldn't let you do all this work alone," Irene informed her younger daughter.

"Besides, we miss being part of the action," Mary Beth admitted. "And the boys were driving us crazy."

"Where's your friend?" Kate asked her mother. Irene had invited a lady from her knitting class.

"Her niece and nephew asked her to join them at the last minute." Irene set down her trademark potato-chip-and-onion casserole, still in its insulated sleeve. "I was looking forward to her company."

Mary Beth was unabashedly opening and closing drawers. "You weren't kidding about this kitchen. I feel like I died and went to heaven."

"Does that mean I'm no longer on a par with Lucifer?" Tony asked, checking the temperature on the turkey.

Kate didn't hear the answer. She had to turn away to hide the strain of another contraction.

Not today. Oh, please, please don't let Tara come today.

"Turkey's done. A hundred and eighty-five degrees, right?" Tony went for the potholders.

"It needs to sit for a while before I carve it." Mary Beth hovered.

"Before who carves it?"

"Oh, you're volunteering? Super."

For the next hour, the pair of them fussed at each other

cheerfully. Potatoes were boiled and mashed, gravy thickened, brown sugar melted on the yams, and Tony, under Mary Beth's supervision, carved the bird with precision.

Kate kept a low profile. She had one more contraction, but amid all the bustle, no one noticed, not even her mother.

On the dot of three o'clock, the chimes rang out musically. In barreled Leo with four pies and what looked like a lifetime supply of whipped cream. A few minutes later, Eve and Hilda appeared, laden with a corn soufflé and baked acorn squash redolent of cinnamon.

"Hilda! I'm so glad to see you," Irene greeted the woman. To the others she said, "Hilda was the real estate agent who sold my house. I've been concerned about her."

"That was shortly after my husband died," Hilda explained. "Irene, have you met Eve? She used to be my foster daughter. Now she's carrying my foster granddaughter, if there is such a word."

"If there's not, there should be," Irene said.

Leo cast a dubious glance from Eve's burgeoning shape to Mary Beth's maternity T-shirt. "Excuse me, how many pregnant women are here?"

"Three," Kate told him.

Leo surveyed the group gathering in the kitchen. "Man, I'm glad I didn't bring a date. It might be catching."

Tony clapped him on the shoulder. "Sorry, little bro. I should have explained the facts of life. After dinner, I'll clue you in."

Everyone laughed except the kids, who were still playing in the storage space. Kate could hear them conducting a mock battle, with Junior giving commands.

The adults carried platter after platter to the dining table. No one could possibly eat that much food, Kate mused.

Her muscles contracted. Not again!

Frantically, she tried to remember what Tina had said about eating and drinking during labor. It was safe in small amounts, but best not to overindulge in case an operation became necessary.

Much as she'd love to believe this would pass, the contractions were coming with greater frequency, about twenty minutes apart. She didn't need to go to the hospital until they reached five minutes, and that might not be for hours.

After the blessing, serving spoons clattered and platters journeyed from hand to hand. The initial confusion subsided once Leo, playing traffic cop, declared that everything be passed clockwise.

Kate put a small slice of meat on her plate. "Is something wrong?" Irene inquired beside her.

Before answering, she glanced around the table. Tony and Leo were debating the comparative merits of the two yam dishes, Mary Beth was dabbing gravy off Johnnie's shirt, and everyone else seemed busy serving or eating.

"I've had a few contractions," Kate murmured. "Rotten timing."

"Might be false labor."

"Doubtful, but it's early. Don't tell anyone."

Her mom nodded. Clearly, she agreed about not spoiling the occasion.

Kate took enough food to avoid further attention. Despite the fabulous scents, though, she didn't have much of an appetite.

Not because of the labor. But because this precious, happy time of her life was ending much too soon.

AFTER DINNER, TONY INSISTED on handling the necessary cleanup, with Leo's help. He shooed most of the group upstairs to inspect the nursery. The decorator's finishing touches included a surveillance camera disguised in a magical forest mural. Kate, too weary for the steps, retired to the family room to keep an eye on the boys, who'd taken over the video game system.

"Never saw this side of you before," Leo said as they divided the food into care packages for their guests.

"Which side?" Tony wondered how much turkey Eve and Hilda would eat. Surely not as much as the Ellroy family, with two growing boys and a dad.

"You're a different person around Kate." His brother stuffed the last spoonful of corn soufflé into his mouth.

"You like her?"

"What's not to like?" Leo responded. "Now, Esther was a piece of work."

"Meaning what?" He had no illusions about the pair being friendly, but he'd never noted any antagonism.

"At your wedding reception, she told everyone I was a detective. Apparently patrolman isn't snazzy enough for her."

That seemed unfair. "Probably a mistake."

"Mind-like-a-steel-trap Esther? Unlikely."

On the point of defending her, Tony subsided. Esther *was* a snob. He'd enjoyed celebrating this holiday without her and her aristocratic parents. "Well, she's gone now."

"Didn't take you long to replace her."

"Excuse me?" He stopped tucking rolls into plastic bags.

"You and Kate have a thing going, right?"

"Only the baby," Tony said. "And once Tara's born…" Suddenly, he wasn't sure how to finish that sentence.

Leo didn't give him a chance, anyway. "Your daughter's name is Tara?"

Of course. He hadn't mentioned it. "You have a problem with that?"

"It surprises me, that's all."

They never talked about their sister, Tony realized, but then, they hadn't talked about much of anything beyond the superficial in years. Hadn't celebrated a Christmas or Thanksgiving together, either. He'd attributed that to Leo's shift schedule, but now he supposed it had something to do with his brother's aversion to Esther. "The name felt right."

"Good. It's time you got past that." Leo carted a stack of dishes to the sink. "You want me to load the dishwasher?"

"Rinse them and leave them. My cleaning crew's coming in tomorrow." There'd been something else he meant to say, before his brother's question about the baby's name. Now, what had they been discussing?

Before he could finish probing the recesses of his brain, his guests trooped in exclaiming over the nursery. "I admire your decorating," Mary Beth told him. "Wish I had a nursery like that. Or, better yet, an extra bedroom. I'm still debating where to put the baby. I'm afraid if I squeeze two boys into the same room, I'll start World War III."

From the den boomed simulated gunfire. "Sounds like you're too late," Hilda said dryly.

"Install bunk beds and tell them they're living in barracks," Leo advised. "Dress them in camouflage, and if they give you a hard time, make them swab out the latrine."

"I love it!" Mary Beth declared. "Hey, even if Tony wants nothing further to do with us, you're welcome at our house anytime, Leo."

"Thanks."

Now Tony remembered what he'd been thinking earlier. After these last few weeks, seeing how smoothly the families blended today, he no longer considered it necessary for him and Kate to avoid each other entirely. He'd draw up a codicil to the surrogacy agreement, allowing her to be involved at some level, perhaps even nurse the baby. Subject to his retaining full custody, of course.

She ought to be thrilled at the idea. He certainly was.

"Where's Kate?" her mother asked.

"In the den." Tony nodded in that direction. "I think she's resting."

"Is she feeling okay?"

"Tired." He shouldn't have left her unattended so long. Perhaps later he could give her a massage, as they'd learned to do in class.

"I'm not leaving this place without seeing the view," Eve announced. "I mean, more than *that*." She waved toward the sunroom's bay window, which provided a glimpse of the backyard and, beyond, a sliver of blue water.

"Fresh air—great idea," Tony said. "I'll switch on the heat lamps and the gas log in the fireplace. Did the boys bring swimsuits?"

"You bet," Mary Beth said. "They can't swim this soon after eating, but I hear tell you have a spa."

"Also a cool collection of miniature sailboats," Tony advised. "We'll leave off the water jets so they can play."

Within minutes, the boys had been rousted and sent to change, while Kate rejoined the group. "You okay?" Tony asked.

"Much better. Tons of energy." She headed into the kitchen before he could stop her. "I'll put on coffee. Leo's working tonight, so he'll need some, and I'll fix a pot of decaf, too. We can eat our pie outside."

Everyone scrambled to help slice the pies, add whipped

cream and carry plates and silverware outside. Within minutes, the stone hearth glowed through the gathering dusk. The boys, more interested in the boats than in dessert, plopped into the spa, while the adults lounged about the deck, enjoying the view of harbor lights and the soothing warmth of heat lamps against the cool evening.

Seated between Hilda and Irene, Leo joked with the two older women. Mary Beth gave Eve practical nursery advice—"You can put a pad on top of the washer-dryer and save the cost of a changing table"—while, next to Tony, Kate stretched out beneath a woven throw.

The murmur of conversation rippled over Tony, enveloping him with a sense of deep satisfaction. This was how he'd imagined this place when he and Esther bought it, as a gathering spot for friends. He'd rather be here right now, with these people, than anywhere in the world.

Beside him, Kate stirred. "Tony?"

He reached for her hand. "Sorry for neglecting you. Feeling better?"

"Well, I hate to bring it up, but…"

The French doors from the house scraped open. Who was left inside? he wondered as he turned.

In the doorway, a queenly figure in a smart, swirling wool dress surveyed the peaceful scene. "Sorry I'm late," declared the woman who ought to be in Washington. "Leo! Great to see you. Is everyone having a wonderful time? Glad we're finally making some use of that fireplace."

"Esther." Tony searched for words to smooth over this unwelcome intrusion and remove his wife without shattering the holiday mood. An impossible task, unfortunately. No one moved Esther anywhere she didn't want to go.

Her glittering eyes skimmed over Mary Beth and Eve, whose maternity tops swelled in the breeze, and fixed on his hand folded over Kate's. "Isn't this an explosion of fertility? How lovely of you to stop by, Mrs. Evans. I hope you're taking good care of my daughter."

Everyone gaped at her. Thanksgiving had just come crashing to a halt.

And much as Tony longed to toss his wife out on her hard, flat butt, he had to grit his teeth and see this through.

Chapter Fifteen

For about ten seconds, Kate tried to hope that Esther was serious about reclaiming the roles of wife and mother that she'd so heedlessly discarded.

No use. She despised the woman, and the contraction racking her midsection did nothing to ease her annoyance. Yet this was Tony's wife. He and only he had the right to deal with her.

Despite Esther's pretense of acting as hostess, none of the adults missed her hostility. Regretfully, they took their leave. The boys toweled off, vocal in their disappointment until Leo bequeathed them each an extra-large portion of pecan and apple pie to take home. Hilda and Mary Beth tucked their care packages into grocery sacks, while Leo set off with two plates of food. One to share with his patrol partner, Kate assumed, but perhaps he planned on eating them both.

Irene took Kate aside. "Are you going to tell him?" she asked.

They both knew that, tonight of all nights, Tony ought to be with Kate. He'd trained as her coach, and she needed his support. But with the contractions still fifteen minutes apart, there was no urgency.

"We can call him later," Kate told her mother. "Plenty of time. Let him deal with this situation now."

While Tony bid his other guests a strained farewell, Kate quietly arranged for her sister to take all three boys home with her. Mary Beth's obvious annoyance with Esther only increased after she learned Kate was in labor, but she held her tongue.

Any last-minute exchange with Tony, even to thank him for hosting the celebration, had to take place under Esther's calculating gaze. How possessive she acted, linking her arm through his and peering down haughtily at "the surrogate." Her arrogance reinforced Kate's decision not to tell her what was happening, because Esther might try to impose her unwelcome presence in the delivery room despite her total lack of preparation.

Perhaps it would serve her right to be present during labor. At one point during Brady's birth, Kate had become so irritable that she'd nearly slapped Quinn. Under the circumstances, no one could blame her if she took a swing at Esther.

Grimly, she pushed aside the idea. The woman was still married to Tony. But the abrupt possibility that Tara might be whisked across the country to a place where Kate would never so much as catch a glimpse of her nearly broke her heart.

Could Esther really still win back her husband? Hard to imagine. Yet Tony had said that, at some level, he didn't feel their marriage was over.

At the door, ignoring his clinging wife, Tony put a hand on Kate's arm. "You forgot your leftovers."

That hadn't been an accident. "I'm stuffed."

"It's not as if we aren't paying her enough to buy food," Esther sniped, no doubt emboldened by the fact that everyone else had left.

Tony jerked his arm loose from his wife's grasp. "That's

incredibly rude, Esther," he snapped. "I'll be right back," he said to Kate.

She didn't object when he returned with several containers of food. She just hoped he hadn't noticed Brady's early departure, and that Irene was lingering outside near Kate's car.

"See you later," she said, accepting the plates and hurrying off before another contraction could give away the game. As for the food, perhaps some anxious dad-to-be at the hospital would enjoy a holiday meal.

Tony's torn expression remained burned in her mind. Surely he'd deal with his wife quickly. Because Kate didn't know how long she could hold out.

Outraged and embarrassed by Esther's behavior, Tony struggled for self-control. Much as he might like to vent, the problem with being married to a shrewd attorney was that she could twist any action or statement to her advantage in court. And if he spoke too harshly, Esther might very well choose to rake him over the coals simply to prove that she could.

What was she after, anyway? She hadn't just dropped in to wish him a happy Thanksgiving.

"What the hell are you doing here?" he asked when they were alone. *Not off to a fine start, are we?*

"I've missed you."

"As I recall, your last words to me were, 'Get that loan, damn it, and don't drag your feet.'"

Esther tossed back her golden brown mane. "Do we have to conduct this conversation in the front hall?"

"Pick any place you like." *How about the nursery, which you didn't bother to fix up?* With an effort, Tony ratcheted down his anger. "You should have let me know you were coming."

"I wasn't sure about the timing. I had dinner with my parents and figured I'd stop by tomorrow. Then I went for a drive and swung by on impulse." She wrinkled her nose at the dining room with its soiled tablecloth and napkins. "Dare I hope for coffee?"

"In the kitchen." He led the way.

When she hesitated by the center island, her unaccustomed air of uncertainty recalled the young woman Tony had known in law school, before she'd become so full of herself. "I apologize for barging in. It didn't occur to me you'd be entertaining. Then when I noticed the cars, I had to find out who was in my house."

Her house. Well, technically, he supposed it was. "Keep going."

"And I guess…" Uncharacteristically, she struggled for words. "When I left, I acted rashly. I was high-handed and arrogant and you have every right to feel betrayed. But I didn't betray you, Tony. There's no other man. You know that, right?"

"Yes. You left me to run your own show, not grab on to someone more important." He poured them each a cup of coffee from the steaming carafe. Other than that, he refused to fall into his usual pattern of playing diplomat.

"You've certainly gotten cozy with the surrogate," she added tightly.

"Someone had to take over the role of birthing coach." He set the cup in front of her.

She didn't respond directly. Instead, she asked, "Who were all those people?"

"Friends." *Mine, not yours.* "Let's get back to the part about you acting arrogant."

She fiddled with a diamond drop earring. "It's lonely in Washington. I wasn't kidding when I said I miss you."

"There's nobody staying up to ask how your court

case went or whisking you to a resort for the weekend because you're working so hard." So much for reining in his resentment.

"You're still mad."

"Don't be silly. A thirty-second apology wipes the slate clean." Sarcasm felt a lot better than it ought to, Tony discovered. "Let me summarize. Once the initial fuss died down, you discovered you're a small fish in an enormous pond filled with barracudas. You flew back expecting adulation and instead ate the usual bleak holiday meal with parents who can't understand why you aren't already running the government. When you stopped by your old house and saw a group of strangers having a terrific time, you couldn't stand it."

"It's not like that. I've been thinking this over for weeks." Esther blinked rapidly. "I made a terrible mistake. You know me, Tony. I get excited when there's something new on the horizon. Is that so terrible?"

"To break your vows and violate my trust? But I guess our marriage wasn't new and exciting enough."

"Hear me out." She wrapped her arms around herself. "I never appreciated how much I relied on you to talk over cases and give feedback on my ideas. You're my coach. It's like that corny song—you're the wind beneath my wings. It came on the radio the other day and I burst into tears. Me! Can you believe it?"

The irony of her using the word *coach* hit hard, considering that she'd abandoned her own commitment to that role. And how doubly ironic that, in her absence he'd come to rely on Kate for feedback and reassurance. Still, his feelings weren't the issue here—Kate's were.

"Some things," he said with deceptive quiet, "aren't about you, Esther. Do you have any idea what this pregnancy means to Kate and her family? She did this as a gift. Never mind the money—you can't buy what she's giving up. You whipped everyone into a frenzy because you wanted what you couldn't have, and then you lost interest."

"And she's cute and domestic and thinks you're wonderful," Esther finished for him. "She's balm for your poor sore heart. I'm not angry that you're a little bit infatuated. But we can start over. We're good together. And we're having a daughter. Isn't that fantastic? What could be better than that?"

Almost anything, Tony answered silently. When Esther first left, he'd hoped for a reconciliation. Now, after enduring weeks of her disdainful indifference, he no longer felt so much as a glimmer of love for her.

More than that, he'd experienced how great it was to bounce *his* ideas off someone and benefit from her insights. To talk and listen and share, instead of always being consigned to the role of backup.

But he had to be careful how he handled this. Esther's mood could turn abruptly, and outright rejection might send her storming vengefully into court. He had to appear to consider her offer, even if that meant spending a few days attempting to work things out until, inevitably, she tired of cooperating and reverted to type.

As for Kate, thank goodness they had a few more weeks before the baby came.

"I DON'T TRUST those fetal monitors," Irene told Kate as they watched the pattern of the baby's heartbeat on the screen. "On TV, a doctor said they sometimes show problems that don't really exist."

"I'd rather take no chances." Kate swallowed hard, and wished for the umpteenth time that Tony were here.

When she'd checked into the labor-and-delivery unit,

the nurse had explained the policy of attaching a belt for about twenty minutes as a precaution to check on the fetal heart rate and contraction pattern. Usually, she'd told Kate and her mother, everything went fine and the belt came off.

But everything wasn't fine. She'd detected an anomaly, whatever that meant, and had ordered an ultrasound.

Tara had to be okay. How could anything go wrong when the baby had passed every checkup with flying colors?

If Tony were around, he'd go marching off in search of the doctor. Kate shuddered. Why did she have to go into labor on a holiday? She'd probably get whatever physician was on duty, possibly a resident.

An aide rolled in an ultrasound device on a cart and left. "Well, guess I won't be needing a refresher course in labor for Mary Beth's baby," Irene commented when they were alone. "Looks like I'm getting my practice today, unless Tony starts answering his phone." She'd left a couple of messages.

"You're supposed to be her coach?"

"Can't count on Ray to be off duty, can we?"

"I hadn't thought of that."

A pinch of pain made Kate tense for another contraction, but she got a brief break. All the more time to wonder what Esther and Tony were discussing at such length.

Oops. It *was* a contraction, and a big one. "Mom!"

"Breathe," her mother instructed. "Huff huff huff."

"It hurts!" She didn't care if she sounded like an infant. At least she wasn't screaming, right? On the other hand, the pain hadn't progressed that far.

"What have we here?" asked a deep masculine voice. "Didn't I mention you're not allowed to go into labor on a holiday?"

"Dr. Rayburn!" Her straining muscles eased at the sight

of the black-haired man with his distinctive thick eyebrows. "How come you're working today?"

"I can't let my favorite patient down." He positioned the ultrasound closer and prepared the paddle.

"I'll bet you say that to all the women," Irene teased.

"Ah, this must be your sister," he observed wryly, drawing a chuckle from his appreciative audience. "Pleased to meet you. Now let's find out what this baby is up to."

He moved the paddle around Kate's bulge. On the monitor, baby limbs went in and out of focus.

"She's okay, isn't she?" Kate asked anxiously.

"Lively and impatient to come out," the obstetrician assured her. "Where's Tony? That rogue's supposed to be helping you."

"Esther showed up at the last minute," she told him. "They're...talking."

Instead of responding, he peered at the screen. "We may have a bit of a situation here."

Kate tried to form a question, but her throat had gone dry. She'd never imagined anything going wrong with this birth. Somehow, being a surrogate seemed like enough of complication.

"Don't keep us in suspense." Irene's voice trembled.

The doctor indicated a ropelike shape. "I don't like the position of the umbilical cord. There's no immediate danger, but I've seen this turn into what we call a cord prolapse. That's when the cord gets trapped as the baby tries to come out, and the pressure reduces or cuts off the oxygen and blood supply."

"That's serious, isn't it?" Kate said. "If the baby lost oxygen for long, the results could be devastating.

"Some doctors will try to reduce the pressure on the cord and deliver vaginally right away." Dr. Rayburn moved the paddle to a different angle, but apparently saw nothing to change his opinion. "I consider that an unnecessary risk. I recommend that we proceed with a cesarean section before the need becomes urgent. After all, your baby's ready to meet the world. What do you say?"

A C-section. Major surgery. Scary, but she trusted Dr. Rayburn. "Yes, if you recommend it. Mom, would you call Tony again?"

"I hate leaving you to go all the way to the lobby," her mother said. Signs warned against using cell phones near monitoring equipment.

"You can call from the patient lounge on this floor." The doctor pointed the way.

After her mother stepped out, Kate blurted the first question that occurred to her. "Am I going to have a big scar across my stomach?"

Dr. Rayburn wiped gel from her abdomen. "Since this isn't an emergency, I can make a transverse cut. You might have heard that referred to as a bikini cut. You'll hardly be able to see it."

That was reassuring. "Can my birth coach be there during the operation?"

"Absolutely. He or she can hold your hand. And you'll be awake when the baby's born, so you won't miss a thing." She'd have to spend an extra few days in the hospital, he added, and take it easy at home for a couple of weeks.

Once Kate ran out of questions, Dr. Rayburn repeated that the baby was fine. He asked a nurse to prep her and called for an anesthesiologist.

Irene returned with the news that she'd left yet another message for Tony. "He's still not answering."

Kate had never considered the possibility of being unable to reach him when she gave birth. "Try again in a few minutes, will you?"

"Sure will." Irene patted her hand. "Women have these

operations all the time. Aren't you lucky your own doctor's available on Thanksgiving?"

"Yes. Very lucky."

The minutes ticked by. Kate signed permission forms, and the anesthesiologist took notes about how much she'd eaten, and the nurses hooked her to an IV.

Tony failed to answer his phone yet again, and again Irene left a message. Kate found herself on a gurney being wheeled to the operating room, with still no sign of him.

Tara's father. The man she loved. Her partner for at least one more precious day.

Why wasn't he here when she needed him most?

Chapter Sixteen

Esther seemed delighted to be back in the house. With the same energy that had propelled her through sixteen-hour days and back-to-back court cases, she roamed the premises as if reclaiming them.

"The fireplace is splendid. How come we hardly ever used it?" she asked, picking up a few overlooked plates on the patio.

"Because we hardly ever entertained." From inside the house, Tony heard the phone ring. For once, he didn't care if the hospital required his services. Whoever it was would have to wait.

"Maybe we could rent out this place instead of selling," she said. "That way, we could afford a nice apartment in D.C. and still come back here if we ever decided to."

"You expect me to move to Washington?" She hadn't mentioned that.

Esther marched inside and piled the dishes on the counter. "If a *man* gets a big break in another city, everyone expects his wife to accompany him."

Tony clenched his teeth with an effort. "And had you brought this up in the first place, I'd have been happy to consider it. Instead, you waved goodbye on your way to the airport. Now you return to scoop me up like a piece of luggage you forgot."

"Would you stop throwing the past at me? I said I was sorry." She dusted off her hands. "What have you done with the nursery? I'm dying to see it."

"Why? You don't plan to live here," he pointed out.

"We can always ship the pieces east."

"Why?" he repeated. "You don't really want a child."

"That's unfair! I love children."

"Do I have to quote what you said about it being my DNA?"

Esther gave a dismissive wave. "That's when I believed we were having a boy, but this is much better. I can buy her clothes, and when she grows up, we'll be best friends."

Was the woman hallucinating? "You skipped something. Like her childhood."

"Of course I'll play with her! I *deserve* a baby."

"In your position, when will you find time to play?" he demanded. "And you got it backwards. A mother doesn't deserve a baby, a baby deserves a mother."

"In D.C., everybody has a nanny. We'll do fine. Anyway, when did you become an expert on child rearing?"

Tony stared at her in dismay. "Quit trying to score points, Esther. We aren't arguing a court case. We're deciding a child's future."

Her foot tapped impatiently against the tile floor. "Come on. Where's the old Tony? We used to be a team."

"That's what I thought, too." He couldn't hold back any longer. "I assumed we were building a future together. It didn't matter to me which of us led or which followed. I figured that, over a lifetime, we'd swap roles whenever it made sense. But there was no team, except in my imagination."

Esther began to pace. "I've never been romantic, Tony. For both our sakes, I wish I were. I shouldn't have walked out. That was stupid. I'm lonely, damn it. There's no reason a woman can't have everything. There's no reason we both can't have everything. Bring the baby, come back with me and I'll prove it."

Behind her, the remains of the feast littered the kitchen where, long ago, he'd pictured the two of them cooking side by side, creating a home. But it wasn't his wife who'd shared that dream today. It was Kate.

The phone rang again. He ignored it. They needed to play this out, here and now.

He had to call Esther's bluff. "Here's the deal. Quit your job, come home and show a commitment to our marriage and our child. Honor your promises. To me, to the baby, to your best friend, who needs your support right now. For once in your life, be there for other people. A year from now, once we've established a real marriage, I'll be willing to consider moving to Washington or wherever you like."

Esther regarded him as if she'd never truly seen him before. What was she thinking?

And what if she said yes?

In the operating room, the nurses set up a screen that prevented Kate from seeing the doctor at work. If she chose to look, a mirror behind him would allow her to see the baby come out.

The anesthetic injected into her spine gave her cold chills. She'd been instructed to hold as still as possible, but she couldn't stop trembling. At least they'd put something in the IV that stopped the contractions and clapped an oxygen mask over her nose and mouth to ensure she took in enough air for the baby.

As Dr. Rayburn began his incision, Irene, covered in scrubs and cap, tried to distract Kate by recounting her last phone conversation with Mary Beth. "The boys are all excited. She was careful to tell them that you're having the baby for Tony, so they won't expect you to bring her home. They insist on seeing her, though, so Mary Beth plans to sneak them into the hospital tomorrow to look in the nursery. It can't hurt, can it? They'll get to see the baby once, anyway."

Maybe I can, too, Kate realized with a spurt of hope. All these months, she'd tried to prepare for the moment when the nurses would hand the baby to the Francos. From the first, Esther had suggested it would be best if she didn't snuggle with the little one, and Kate—not yet pregnant, and thrilled by the idea of sharing a miracle with this nice couple—had agreed.

She must have been out of her mind.

What a paradox. She longed to see Tony, and yet a small part of her rejoiced that, in his absence, she might be able to hold Tara. For a few precious moments, she could see the small angel that she'd been carrying.

Then she heard a familiar male voice say, "No, I'm not her husband, I'm the baby's father." Her heart leaped. In spite of everything, she longed for Tony's strength.

"Let him in," Dr. Rayburn instructed whoever was blocking Tony's path. "I'll vouch for him."

A moment later, brilliant green eyes peered into Kate's. The cap covering his hair emphasized the strong line of Tony's jaw, with a hint of late-day stubble. "How're you doing?" He touched her cheek lightly. "Can't talk, huh? Guess I can make jokes at your expense, then."

"If you make my patient laugh, I'll throw you out," the doctor threatened.

"Better than firing me," Tony returned. To Kate, he said, "Sorry I'm late."

What happened with Esther? She willed him to answer.

Telepathy, however, didn't seem to be his forte, because he turned and thanked Irene for leaving him messages.

"It never occurred to me she'd gone into labor," he explained. "I should have picked up the phone. When I finally heard what you said about the surgery, I broke the speed limit and possibly the sound barrier."

"Good thing your brother didn't give you a ticket," Irene said tartly.

"Leo? He'd have provided me a police escort."

Kate felt a tugging in her abdomen. Abruptly, the mood in the operating room changed. Everyone fell silent, staring as the doctor lifted out the baby. She caught only a glimpse above the screen before a nurse took the infant and handed her to another figure in scrubs. Dr. Sellers, the neonatologist. Kate hadn't seen him come in.

A loud squall produced a ripple of relieved conversation. "She's got quite a set of lungs!" someone said.

"Good color," a nurse observed.

"She's gorgeous." Tony vibrated as if preparing to launch himself into orbit.

"Red and covered with goop and squinting," Irene teased.

"Perfect," he answered, and no one disagreed.

Kate's heart throbbed. *Let me have her.* But no one reacted.

Tears rolled down her cheeks. After all she'd been through today, she didn't even get to hold her daughter. She ached to see that tiny red face, and those beautiful squinty eyes. For nearly nine months, she and Tara had been one flesh, one being, one magically bonded soul, and now they were separated forever.

"Hey." It was Tony, back again, his thumb collecting a teardrop. "Don't cry."

A nurse lifted off the oxygen mask, but Kate still

couldn't speak. She turned her head away. Wasn't the anesthesiologist supposed to give her a sedative that would make her sleepy? If only she could blot out this scene.

"You're going to have to help me with this." What was Tony talking about? She blinked, and gazed up blearily.

He stood over her holding a small blanket-wrapped bundle, a nightcap on her head and feet covered with the cutest little socks. "Tara?" Kate whispered.

Instead of answering, Tony addressed the baby. "Your mommy wants you. I'll place you on her chest, and she'll tell you how much trouble you gave her."

The tears kept flowing, but these were tears of joy. She did get to hold Tara. And to touch Tony's hands as, together, they welcomed their baby.

KATE WOKE UP ALONE. Morning light played across the hospital room and the other empty bed. Vaguely, she recalled spending a short while in the recovery unit, and then being moved here. The rest of the night had passed in a sedated haze.

She didn't see a bassinet, but then, she hadn't really expected Tony to let her bring the baby into her room. It had been enough just to share that special moment.

What idiocy. It hadn't been anywhere near enough. Now they were gone, both of them. Her daughter and her…and Tony.

He'd never told her what had happened with Esther, Kate realized. But then, his life wasn't her business anymore.

She hated the fact that she was crying again. Tears defied her, though, sliding down and dampening the pillow. Thank goodness she didn't have a roommate. Seeing another woman and her family rejoicing over a baby would have been more than Kate could bear.

A tap at the door drew her attention. Mary Beth gave

her a bittersweet smile. "Can we come in? We've all been down to the nursery. She's amazing."

Quickly, Kate wiped her tears. From behind Mary Beth, Brady dodged into the room and raced to the bedside. "Why do you have wires on you, Mommy? Can I climb up?"

"Don't jostle her," warned Irene, shepherding in Junior and Johnnie. Following her stern instructions, the two older boys settled on chairs.

"Sit next to me on the chair, sweetie," Kate told her son. "This isn't a wire; it's a tube called an IV. It gives me water and medicine. I'm sure they'll take it out soon."

Everyone had questions—How did she feel? Had she heard any more from the Francos?—but underneath, she felt a current of sadness. They all longed to keep the baby, Kate more than anyone.

Could this really be over? Did Tony truly intend to take Tara and exit from Kate's life?

I love him. But he had a wife. And with his kind heart, if Esther had come back to beg forgiveness, he'd probably give her a second chance.

"I wish we weren't flying out of town today to see Ray's parents," Mary Beth fretted. "We've got to be at the airport in a couple of hours."

Irene patted her older daughter's arm. "Brady and I will have lots of fun, and you'll be back Sunday, in plenty of time to take Kate home from the hospital." She turned to her younger daughter. "They aren't letting you out before then, are they?"

"I doubt it."

At a stir in the doorway, Kate felt a lurch of wild joy. Tony…but no, it was Dr. Rayburn. Still, she found his presence a comfort.

"Oh, it's the doctor," Mary Beth said. "Guess that's our

signal to leave. Brady, the doctor needs to be alone with your mom."

"Don't forget, we're going to have the house to ourselves," Irene reminded her grandson. "You can play Dance Dance Revolution all you like. For lunch, how about macaroni and cheese?"

"Yay!" He stood on tiptoe to give Kate a kiss. "Get better quick, Mommy."

"I will."

After everyone left, Dr. Rayburn examined the incision and reviewed Kate's vital signs. "Everything looks good. The nurses should have you on your feet and taking a few steps this morning. How're you doing otherwise?"

She didn't have to keep up her guard with him about the surrogacy. "It's harder than I expected."

"This is an unusual situation," Dr. Rayburn conceded. "I've dealt with these arrangements before, and usually everything goes smoothly."

In the hallway, Kate heard a cart roll by. It stopped, and to her astonishment, a nurse's aide wheeled in a bassinet. "This can't be Tara."

As the aide positioned the newborn beside the bed, Dr. Rayburn checked the plastic bracelet. "Baby Girl Evans."

Evans, not Franco? Kate remembered that the hospital always labeled babies with the mother's last name for ease of tracking. "Did they bring her in by mistake?"

"No, I don't believe so." The doctor winked. "I'll see you tomorrow." He finished making a note on her chart and went out.

Her heart racing, Kate scooted awkwardly into a sitting position and reached to stroke the newborn. She didn't dare lift Tara by herself yet, and the aide had left along with the obstetrician.

When she caught a whiff of familiar aftershave, every nerve cell in her body quivered. Kate stared in disbelief at the man strolling through the door wearing a wry, tender smile. He'd come, after all. He hadn't abandoned her.

"We have a lot to talk about," Tony said.

Chapter Seventeen

Curious as she was about Esther, Kate wished Tony would sweep her into his arms and say sweet, loving things. Right now, she didn't care what his wife had wanted or what tactic he'd used, as long as he was here. She wanted to bury her face in his tan corduroy jacket and simply inhale him.

Yet he seemed determined to tell her the whole story, and to keep a slight distance as he outlined Esther's request for reconciliation. "She seemed to believe Tara and I would accessorize her new life quite nicely."

Kate could hardly bear to listen. She wasn't ready to hear bad news or deal with its aftermath. "Would you hand me the baby?"

"You mean...pick her up?" From his tone, she might have been requesting he defuse a nuclear bomb.

"You did it last night."

"The nurse set her in my arms," he admitted.

Kate had to smile. "Remember what they showed us in class? Be sure to support her head."

Tony approached the bassinet. Instantly, his tone softened. "Hi, baby girl. She looks hungry, don't you think?"

"Newborns usually lose a few ounces the first day,"

Kate reminded him, since that was another point Tina had covered. "Hold on. I need to get ready."

"For what?"

"To nurse." She fumbled with the front of her hospital gown.

Tony turned bright red. "Listen, Kate, that's great, but can you wait? I'd like to finish our conversation without... distractions."

"Sure." Disappointed, she retied the laces. "So, Esther wants..." She let the words trail off.

"Everything, like she always does." He shook his head. "I insisted she quit her job and act like a real wife and mother for a year. You should have seen how fast she headed for the door. It's over between us."

She clung to his words. "You're getting a divorce? It's settled?"

"As soon as we can get a judge's approval."

Kate sagged against the pillow. Finally.

"The whole time she was trying to win me back, I couldn't stop thinking how much I've enjoyed being around you and Brady." His full mouth curved. "Everything's changed this past month. *I've* changed."

She could hardly breathe. *Tell me you love me.*

"Thanksgiving helped me understand that Tara deserves a family, not just a father," Tony went on. "A grandmother, cousins, people to celebrate with."

"And a mother," Kate said more eagerly than she intended.

Reaching into the bassinet, Tony took his daughter's tiny hand. "Cutting you out of her life would be cruel."

She wished he wouldn't choose his words so carefully. *Just tell me!* "What do you mean?"

Tony cleared his throat. "I stayed up half the night, trying to work out an amendment to the surrogacy arrangement

that would be fair to everyone. Here's what I've come up
with so far. I'd greatly appreciate if you would agree to
nurse her for at least a few months. I'd retain custody, of
course, but you and Brady could stay at my house. After
that..."

Nurse her for a few months? Move into his house with
Brady to suit Tony's convenience?

Maybe Kate had been a fool to hope for more, but she'd
certainly never expected to be treated like this. "What do
you take me for, a nanny?"

He stiffened. "I'm trying to be reasonable."

Kate had run out of patience. Maybe Tony didn't love
her, but he certainly owed her more than a job as a disposable nursemaid. "I'll tell you what's reasonable. If you love
your daughter, you'll share custody with me. You'll make
a great dad, but you aren't prepared to raise her alone."

"Need I remind you that you signed..."

"You've done nothing *but* remind me of that since your
wife dumped you!" she flared. "My sister's been telling
me all along that genetic mothers have legal rights. Don't
make me fight you. That will hurt us both."

His face tightened. "You're going back on your
word?"

"With you offering me the post of wet nurse-in-
residence? I've never been so insulted, even by Esther."

His disapproval shifted to uncertainty. "I didn't mean
it that way, Kate. You aren't the hired help, for pity's sake.
You're special to me. And you're Tara's mother. There's no
reason we can't share her on a daily basis. I've got plenty
of room for you and Brady both."

"We have our own house. I'm not uprooting my son for
some temporary arrangement."

"Well, if things work out, maybe we can—"

"Do what?" She was so angry, her stitches hurt. "Hang

out as roommates until you find the woman of your dreams?" She hadn't forgotten Mary Beth's reminder that someday he would remarry a new and improved version of Esther.

"Where is this coming from?"

With an effort, Kate reined in her temper. "You said once that you believe in marriage. Well, so do I. What should I tell my son if I move in with a man, and I'm neither an employee nor a wife?"

"I wasn't suggesting that kind of arrangement."

"You might as well have. It's what everyone would assume." She stopped short of pointing out the obvious— that they weren't likely to keep their hands off each other for long.

"Kate, what's the problem here? We've always been able to discuss things."

"You figure it out." Oh, blast, she was crying again.

Tony stood there looking so bewildered that she nearly forgave him. But not quite. How could she have so completely misread their interaction these past weeks? Did he truly feel nothing for her?

The silence lengthened. Just when she thought his reserve might break down at last, he said, "I'll send someone in to help you with the baby."

Kate wished she had a shoe to throw at the door as he left. Or that she hadn't shut him out. That she'd told him… What?

That she loved him too much to accept anything less than marriage? He'd made it clear that wasn't on the table. In fact, he'd probably be shocked to learn she dared see herself in that role.

A moment later, as he'd promised, the aide came in. With her help, Kate brought Tara to her breast.

Whatever else happened, she decided as she nursed, she'd done one thing right today. She'd decided to fight for her baby, no matter what it cost.

ANGER KICKED IN as Tony drove home. How dare Kate change the rules and throw them in his face? He hadn't meant to insult her. If anything, he'd paid her the respect of believing she would keep her word about their agreement.

What was so complicated about the fact that people required guidelines and boundaries? That was why civilized societies had laws. That was what kept everyone safe.

He arrived home to find the cleaners, who had a key, vacuuming the last of yesterday's celebration from the carpet. The dining room had been restored to its customary spotless state, as had the kitchen. They'd aired out the place, as well, removing the lingering scents of sage and cinnamon that he'd inhaled when he came downstairs this morning.

Tony wished they'd put everything back. He didn't want Thanksgiving obliterated. He yearned to live it over and over, to dwell in that happy time when things still made sense.

He wrote out a check and wished the crew a happy holiday. Cheerfully, they finished mopping the entryway and headed to their van.

Leaving him alone. For once, it didn't seem like such a treat to have the holiday weekend free.

Tony wandered through the house, scarcely seeing the sunlight sparkling through the wide rear windows and on the harbor far below. He wanted Kate here. It had seemed so obvious and inevitable that she and Brady should move in. Last night when, too restless to sleep, he'd strolled from his bedroom to the nursery, he'd pictured her standing by the crib, hair flowing around her shoulders, her face glowing at the sight of him.

What do you take me for, a nanny?

Of course he hadn't meant that. She was so much more. That's what made it difficult to work out the new rules.

She'd been right about the legalities. Tony had to admit that, despite their contract, the law granted the mother certain rights until she formally relinquished them after the baby's birth. His only recourse would be to withhold the final payment, but he couldn't in good conscience deprive her and Brady of that.

Damn it, he'd been fair and honest every step of the way. If he'd insulted her, it was by accident. Perhaps he should simply suggest that they renegotiate their agreement. That sounded less arbitrary than presenting her with a preconceived plan.

Other than that, he had no idea how to proceed. Maybe she'd be calmer today. He desperately hoped so.

That afternoon, Tony returned to the hospital. At the nursery, he held Tara and crooned to her, thrilled at the way she responded to his voice. For those few minutes, nothing else mattered.

But afterwards, when he went to see Kate, her mother stopped him outside the door. "She's upset with you," Irene said bluntly.

"We can work this out like mature adults," Tony told her.

"You're talking about a business negotiation?"

"More or less." From inside the room, he heard Kate reading to Brady. Like gently rippling water, her voice soothed Tony's spirit.

"A hospital room isn't a good place to conduct business," the older woman advised. "I suggest you wait until she's released on Sunday."

"Before then, we'll need to decide who's taking the baby home," he pointed out.

Irene held firm. "I suspect the hospital will release Tara to her mother. Or are you going to make a stink about that?"

Tony supposed he might prevail, but creating a scene would only antagonize Kate further. And it just plain felt wrong to take the child against her mother's will. "No."

"Then this can all be dealt with next week. Until then, my daughter's no longer in your employ, so to speak." She might look frail, but steel underlay Irene's words.

Tony thanked her and left, determined to try again tomorrow when he came to visit Tara. No longer in his employ? Kate couldn't believe that was all that lay between them.

He no longer knew where he stood on anything, Tony realized as he exited the hospital. For five years, his life had moved along smoothly, and then, in the past two months, everything had fallen apart. What if he leaped to a decision, only to discover it was the wrong one?

He had to take this one step at a time.

On Saturday morning, Tony found Tara's bassinet missing from the nursery. As he approached Kate's room, he could hear Eve and Hilda chattering away inside. Frustrated at being unable to talk to Kate alone, he marched out to his car and began to drive.

He'd always preferred to solve his problems by thinking them through on his own. Now that technique failed utterly. He needed advice. But the person he yearned for, the person whose opinion mattered most, apparently no longer wished to speak to him.

Tony slowed as he passed Kate's house. Even in November, roses flourished in the yard of the old-fashioned bungalow. He missed his best friend with a pain as sharp as a scalpel.

A few blocks farther, he discovered he was approaching Leo's place. Tony hadn't visited here since he and Esther attended his brother's housewarming party four years ago. Afterwards, on the way home, Esther had regaled him with bitingly funny remarks about his brother's beer-hall décor. Until she mentioned it, Tony hadn't paid much attention to the linoleum flooring in the den, the Coca-Cola stained-glass lamps or the pool table. Leo was a bachelor, after all.

On impulse, Tony parked in front of his brother's house. No carefully tended roses here. Whoever mowed the lawn had simply taken the tops off the weeds rather than removing them, and a rectangular evergreen hedge squatted sullenly beside the porch.

The buzzer quickly brought Leo, his jaw covered with stubble and his faded T-shirt advertising a surfing contest. "Hey," he said by way of greeting. "I'm guessing the witch got on her broom and flew back to D.C., because she'd never have let you come over here."

"Good to see you, too." From the interior, Tony noted the blare of a football game.

"Come on in." Leo ushered him inside, where, to Tony's surprise, a stocky woman with stick-straight blond hair lounged on the couch, her feet plopped on the coffee table and a plate of pecan pie in her lap.

"I hope I'm not interrupting anything," Tony said.

She muted the TV. "Naw. Our team's losing anyway."

"Tony, this is my partner, Patty. Patty, meet my bro."

Partner? Tony gave her a friendly nod. "I didn't realize you were dating someone, Leo. You should have invited Patty to Thanksgiving."

The woman snorted. "Dating? He's my *patrol* partner."

Ah. That explained why he hadn't mentioned her.

"Patty lives down the street," Leo explained.

"I see."

"Thanks for sending home all that turkey," Patty added. "I spent Thanksgiving with my hippie parents in Tucson, eating tofurkey and bean sprouts. If it weren't for Leo, I'd starve."

"Patty's strictly a burgers-and-fries kind of gal," his brother noted.

"If you can't grill it or fry it, I'll pass." She waved her fork. "I make an exception for pie."

"Something we can help you with?" Leo asked Tony.

He could hardly ask his brother for advice in front of this stranger. "Well, first of all, congratulations. You're an uncle."

"Hurrah for me," Leo deadpanned. "And?"

"Kate and I are having a slight disagreement."

"About the surrogacy business?" Obviously Patty had heard about it. "She's one hell of a gal, Tony. What's that old saying? Don't throw out the baby with the bathwater. Well, you could learn something from that."

"What, exactly?" Leo asked.

Tony ignored his brother's sarcasm. "You know Kate?" he asked Patty.

"We met. She was helping that young kid. Eve." She downed a last bite of pie before continuing. "So are you in love with her or what?"

Leo shot his partner a warning glance. "Patty…"

"Sorry." She set the empty plate aside. "I'll let you guys talk this out. Thanks for the eats. Nice to meetcha, Tony." Out she sauntered.

After the door closed behind her, Leo said, "It's almost

too bad you're divorcing Esther. I'd like to see her and Patty square off one of these days."

"Why? I got the impression you like Patty."

"I do. I'm just into blood sports."

Time to come to the point. "I need feedback. Obviously, I'm desperate, because I'm asking you."

"Compliments like that could go to a fellow's head." Leo flopped on the couch, into the spot probably still warm from his partner's behind. "What are you and Kate fighting about?"

Tony did his best to sum up their discussion. "She's really angry, and I'm not sure what to do," he concluded.

"I'd guess she wants more than a temporary position. As Patty said, are you in love with her or what?"

"It's not that simple." Tony tried to marshal his thoughts. "I'm not even divorced yet. Besides, we signed a contract."

"Burn it."

What kind of anarchy was his brother advocating? "We've got a daughter to raise. We need ground rules."

"Ground rules?" Leo scoffed. "Marry her."

If Kate would agree, that sounded like a dream…but dreams had a way of blowing up in your face unless you were prepared. "This is all new. We have to take it slow."

"The idea of falling madly in love scares the hell out of you, doesn't it?"

"You're confusing caution with fear. Remember, I married Esther."

"Esther wasn't the love of your life, she was an investment," his brother said. "Go on, tell me she broke your heart when she left."

Stunned him, yes. But in all honesty… "No."

"You asked for my advice. Here it is." In Leo's intense gaze, Tony suddenly saw not his kid brother but a veteran police officer. "Every day, people take chances and lose. They misjudge a traffic light and get killed, or trust their retirement savings to a guy who blows it in Las Vegas. Once, I nearly shot a guy I thought was holding a gun. What stopped me? Not any genius on my part. It was a cell phone and it rang. Sometimes you get lucky. Other times, life smashes you in the face. What you don't do is waste your life trying to hang on to the illusion that you're in control."

"Are you talking about Esther?" Tony asked in confusion.

"I'm talking about our sister."

A chill crept over him. Not the coolness of this November day, but the late-afternoon sea breeze of fifteen years ago. The breeze he'd ignored because for once he and Tara had thrown off their parents' restrictions and defied the rules. That day at the beach, his sister had laughed freely. That day, they'd taken a chance on life.

That day, Tony had killed the person he loved most in the world.

Chapter Eighteen

On Sunday morning, Dr. Rayburn pronounced Kate well enough to go home. "What about Tara?" she asked anxiously. "Can she come with me?"

She hadn't heard from Tony since their confrontation on Friday. The argument had played through Kate's mind repeatedly, in so many versions that she no longer recalled exactly what either of them had said. He'd been angry.... He'd been apologetic.... She'd been justifiably furious.... She'd gone off the deep end....

According to her mother, he'd dropped by later that day, but she'd told him Kate hadn't been up to a rematch. She'd expected him to return later. Why hadn't he?

She'd probably alienated him forever. In her worst imaginings, she saw him scooping up Tara and refusing to allow further visits until they battled each other in court. Even if she won, she'd lose, financially and emotionally.

At other times, she let herself picture him falling onto his knees and making a passionate declaration of love. But as the hours ticked by, and Friday turned into Saturday, that faint hope had faded. Now it was Sunday.

Physically, she was healing from the surgery. Walking, eating normally, gaining strength. Yet being released from the hospital seemed as if it would sever the last connection between her and Tony, sending them out to lead their separate lives. Still, what about their daughter?

Dr. Rayburn finished leafing through her chart. "Since I don't see a court order requiring me to turn the baby over to her father, she can go home with you. I'll tell the nursery to get her ready. Do you have some household help for the next few days?"

"My mother's going to sleep over until Wednesday or Thursday." Although Irene insisted she'd be fine on the couch, Kate hated to make her mother uncomfortable any longer than necessary.

"Excellent. For the first month, don't lift anything heavier than the baby," he warned. "No stairs, and no driving until your six-week checkup." He told her to contact him immediately in case of fever or heavy bleeding. "And don't hesitate to call if you suffer from negative feelings. Depression affects some new mothers, regardless of their situation."

"And mine's far from ideal," Kate noted. "I'll keep that in mind."

She managed a smile, despite the ache at losing Tony. Hadn't she been aware all along that she wasn't the type of woman he could fall in love with?

"I'll see you in six weeks, then." After advising that a nurse would come in soon to arrange her discharge, the doctor wished Kate well and left.

She tried to brace for this transition. Earlier, her mom had phoned to say Mary Beth's family was back with lots of anecdotes about their second Thanksgiving. After church, Irene planned to bring Brady to the hospital to collect Kate and Tara. Tonight, she'd be in her own bed, home with her son and, apparently, with her daughter, too.

Yet nothing felt right.

When the door opened, Kate glanced up blearily,

expecting the nurse. Her heart leaped at the sight of Tony in a navy blue sweater and slacks. His eyes were forest-dark, and faint lines etched the corners of his mouth.

Her joy constricted to panic. "You've come to take Tara."

"What?" He gave a start. "No."

Without waiting for an invitation, he moved to the edge of her bed. As his weight shifted the mattress and his strong hand cupped hers, Kate relished his spicy scent and the warmth of his skin. She arched toward him instinctively. "I didn't mean to make you so angry the other day."

"No angrier than I made you. We're both over it, I trust." He showed no sign of relaxing, however. "There's something I need to share with you."

Not another contract modification. Still, she'd better not jump the gun. "Yes?"

"I told you about my sister, Tara—that she had spina bifida," he began.

Was he concerned that their daughter had inherited a genetic defect? "But our little girl's fine."

"Yes. I'm talking about her namesake. I want you to understand...." He broke off as if the words stuck in his throat.

The bleakness on his face disturbed her. What on earth was the matter? "Go on."

As he struggled for words, she saw the weariness beneath the well-groomed surface. He must have lain awake half the night.

Finally he spoke. "I killed her."

"You did what?" He couldn't have. "I don't believe it."

"Not intentionally," he conceded.

"Whatever you did, you've obviously carried a big load of

guilt all these years." Now she understood his haunted air. But what made him take on such heavy responsibility?

"Tara used to catch colds and flu easily," Tony said hoarsely. "To keep her safe, our parents hired a tutor and schooled her at home. Outings were restricted to locations like museums, on days when attendance would be light. No amusement parks, no shopping malls, no large birthday parties. She was allowed only a few carefully screened friends. As you might guess, the older she got, the more she chafed at the restrictions."

"What a tough situation." While Kate would do anything to protect her children, she empathized with Tara, too.

"I became her ally." Tony stretched his legs across the floor. "After I turned sixteen—when she was ten—I was able to drive her places. I'd promise our parents to take her to an art exhibit, for instance. We'd spend ten minutes there and then sneak off to the movies. Once, we went to a toy store. You should have seen the way she ran her hands over the stuffed animals and the dolls. She loved spending her Christmas money on things she could touch and examine. Of course, we hid the stuff in a trunk, and later claimed she'd ordered it on the Internet."

"How sweet." *What a compassionate brother.*

His spark of pleasure dimmed. "The summer she turned eleven, Dad had an out-of-town conference and, for once, Mom went with him. They trusted me to supervise Tara for a few days while they were gone."

From the corridor, Kate heard footsteps. She caught her breath, fearing an intrusion, but whoever it was continued on.

"She begged me to take her to the beach. When she was little, she'd been allowed to play in the sand a few times, until she got a nasty sunburn that became infected." His voice grew thick. "I'm not sure whether Mom forgot the sunscreen or it simply washed off, but our parents would never risk it again. Anyway, Tara was always watching beach scenes on TV. Teenage romance, that kind of thing. She pleaded with me to take her."

"What could it hurt?" Kate sympathized.

"That's what I thought. Because I did so well at school and stayed out of trouble, people considered me practically a grown-up. But at seventeen, I didn't have mature judgment."

A sense of dread rippled through her. "What went wrong?"

"She had a slight cold, but she'd been so healthy for months that neither of us thought much of it," Tony said. "We had a great time. Yes, I remembered the sunscreen. And we arrived around three o'clock, when the sun wasn't so harsh. But I forgot how cold the sea wind can be, even in summer."

"She caught a chill," Kate surmised.

A muscle twitched in his jaw. "We bought fried clams at a stand, and ate supper there. Then I noticed she was shivering. I wrapped her in a blanket and took her home."

She could sense the painful images replaying in his mind. "And then?"

"The next morning, when I went to fetch her for breakfast, she was burning with fever. I called an ambulance while Leo tracked down our parents by phone. She had pneumonia, Kate." His voice broke. "I had no idea she could get so sick, so fast. She couldn't fight it off, even with medicine. Two days later, she died. I didn't believe it. Sometimes I still can't."

"Your parents blamed you?"

He released a long breath. "No more than I blamed myself."

"And you've lived with the remorse ever since?"

"I tried to put it behind me." He folded his arms across his chest. "My parents forgave me. They said they shouldn't have put so much responsibility on a teenager. But Mom—it was as if she lost the will to live. A year later, she got cancer. After she died, Dad remarried and I guess he was happy enough, but he died of a stroke the year I finished law school. We never had a chance to connect as adults."

"I'm sorry." How strange to discover such sorrow beneath Tony's confident manner.

"I came to terms with the situation by taking control—of everything. I'd broken the rules once and my sister paid with her life. At some level I resolved never to make that mistake again. A legal career suited me perfectly. And although it wasn't a conscious decision, I married a woman who saw life the same way. I felt safe as long as we both knew where the lines were. It was a delusion, of course."

She had no idea why he'd decided to open up to her now, but thank goodness he had. "I'm glad you told me."

"So am I. Kate…"

This time, the footsteps in the hall didn't continue on. Instead, a nurse entered briskly, carrying a clipboard and a sheaf of papers. "Mrs. Evans? I have your discharge instructions."

Kate cast an apologetic glance at Tony. She could hardly order the woman to go away. "Is my family here?"

"Just your husband." The woman indicated Tony. Obviously, not everyone on the staff recognized the hospital's attorney.

He roused as if emerging from a dream. "If it's all right, Kate, I'll be driving you home. I phoned your mother and arranged for her and Brady to meet you at your house."

"Well…sure." What was this about, anyway?

She didn't get to ask, because the nurse stayed to help

her put on her street clothes, and then a volunteer popped in with a wheelchair. "I can walk," Kate protested.

"Hospital policy," Tony advised. "We don't want patients tripping on their way out. People tend to be a little unsteady on their feet. I sound like a damn lawyer, don't I?"

"There's a reason for that."

He slanted her a grin. "Well, I don't have to sound like one all the time."

A second volunteer arrived, pushing Tara in her bassinet. "Let's check those plastic bracelets one more time." She compared them. "Yep. Just cut these off with scissors when you get home."

How incredible that this tiny girl, with her bright eyes and red cheeks, belonged to them. Even though she'd taken her son home five years ago, the experience felt just as new and miraculous this time.

When Tony bent to kiss his daughter's forehead, she cooed gleefully. "You are such a doll," he told her. "Your parents are going to spoil you rotten."

With a third volunteer handling the bouquets sent by well-wishers, they formed a parade down the hall, into the elevator and through the lobby. Several doctors and nurses greeted Tony, admired Tara and congratulated Kate.

"Thanks, everyone. Sorry we can't stay and chat." With that response, Tony put the parade in motion again.

At the entrance, Kate spotted Tony's car parked in a restricted zone. "Special privileges?"

"Absolutely." He shepherded the little group across the walkway and plucked a placard from the windshield. "Courtesy of the administrator."

"And here I figured it's because I'm such a great mom."

"That, too."

While a volunteer loaded the flowers into the trunk,

Tony eased Kate into the front seat, then strapped Tara in the rear infant seat. With a jolt, she recalled fantasizing about this moment when he took them both home from the hospital.

Could this be a dream come true? Or was she headed for another letdown?

RELIVING THAT DAY WITH TARA had been agonizing for Tony. Oddly, though, as he told the story to Kate, he'd seen it through fresh eyes. A seventeen-year-old boy filled with good intentions, believing his sister as invincible as he felt himself. Two kids having a great time, blissfully unaware they were awakening a deadly monster.

Maybe her cold would have turned into pneumonia and killed her anyway, and she'd have missed that glorious day at the beach. You didn't get to know these things in advance, Tony mused. You had to take life the best way you could and accept the consequences.

Amazing how much he was still learning at the age of thirty-two. Now, he couldn't wait to get Kate home and finish their discussion.

For heaven's sake, why did they have to hit traffic on a Sunday? They should have zipped over to her house in five minutes, but, ahead, emergency lights flashed at the intersection. Apparently an accident had gridlocked the cars on Safe Harbor Boulevard. Sitting on a cross street, Tony glanced around to see if he could back up and turn around.

No room to maneuver. Irked, he drummed his palms against the steering wheel.

"What's the hurry?" Kate asked.

"I have this whole…" *I have this whole thing mapped out.* An agenda. An organized case to present to a one-woman jury.

"This whole what?" she pressed.

Instead of a direct answer, Tony heard himself say, "Brady left a toy car in the sunroom."

"I'm sorry."

"No, no, that's not the point." Even though he was going about this all wrong, he plowed ahead. "When I saw it this morning, I felt like he ought to be there with me. He belongs in my house."

"Brady?" Kate asked uncertainly.

"That stuffing you made for Thanksgiving. It's delicious, all those flavors blending together." He knew he was rambling on, but was unable to stop. "I ate some cold for breakfast, pacing around the deck. Remember what a great time we had out there?" The traffic inched forward. Ahead, a cop was waving vehicles across the boulevard, and Tony tapped the gas a little too hard. He braked inches from the next car's bumper.

"I'll be happy to give you the recipe."

"For what?"

"The stuffing."

"I don't want the recipe, I want you," Tony blurted. "Oh, rats." Did the cop have to halt them *now?*

"You do?" she asked breathlessly.

He tried once again to organize his thoughts, but now that he'd opened the floodgates, out they spilled. "You belong with me. At your place, my place, the middle of the street, the hospital lobby, wherever. You're the sunlight on my face, the air that I breathe." How could something so maudlin be true?

"That's poetic," Kate murmured.

"I'm never poetic. I'm not sure what I'm talking about." Tony grimaced as a fire truck dislodged from its spot on the boulevard ahead of them, opening a gap at last. Now where was that officer? It appeared he'd abandoned them to a signal light stuck permanently on red.

"Quit staring at the signal and talk to me," Kate urged.

"I love you." He hadn't approached this right. Tony gestured behind him. "If you look in my briefcase, you'll find my copy of the surrogacy contract. I planned to hand it over before I brought this up, along with a check for the rest of what I owe you, so we could start with a level playing field. I've done it backwards. If you'll give me a chance…"

"I love you, too."

She'd spoken without hesitation. She hadn't tried to bargain, despite the fact that he'd put her in a perfect position to demand whatever she wanted.

Because she's Kate, not Esther. How insane that he'd spent years with a woman who calculated every move. "You're nothing like my wife," he marveled. "I mean, my almost ex-wife."

"I know I'm not a high-powered attorney or anything. I'll never have a prestigious job or impress people." The words trembled in the air.

She'd misunderstood, and then—blast it—the signal went green and he had to shoot forward or risk getting stuck here for another eternity. Tony needed to focus on his driving, to protect his precious cargo. "Can we finish this discussion at your place?"

"Sure." She bit her lip.

Wishing the car had wings instead of tires, Tony tapped the gas pedal again and finally, finally made it through the intersection.

Chapter Nineteen

Tony seemed so agitated and then, for the rest of the short drive to Kate's house, he stopped speaking entirely. She hardly dared to trust her rising hope.

He'd said he loved her, and made that poetic declaration about the air he breathed and the sunlight on his face. But then he'd started talking about the contract and she was afraid he'd regretted his words.

In the rear seat, Tara appeared contented with her first taste of the outside world. For this moment, the three of them formed a family. If only they could run into another traffic jam so Kate could treasure this moment a little longer.

Too soon, they stopped in front of her house. From the porch, a flock of pink balloons bobbed on a tether, while in the yard a pink placard declared: "Welcome, baby girl!"

"Did you do that?" she asked in surprise.

"Sneaked over this morning," Tony said.

"It's great." What a sweet touch.

"Nothing fancy, but the only store I found open was a pharmacy, and they had a limited selection." He switched off the ignition. "Let's get back to what you were saying about her majesty Queen Esther."

Kate's stomach tightened. "I didn't mean..."

"You outshine her in every way." Tony spoke low and

earnestly. "I don't just love you, Kate, I admire you. I admire your strength, the way you anchor your family. The way you're willing to yield when it's called for, or stick up for what's right. The way you think of others while staying true to yourself. You're the toughest, most loving woman I've ever met. I can't draw lines between us anymore, because you and the kids are everything to me." His eyes shone with emotion.

Kate could scarcely breathe. "Oh, Tony."

"I've got… Hang on." He snagged his briefcase from the floor behind her seat.

"We don't have to deal with the contract right now."

"There's this other thing." From inside the case, he retrieved a long jeweler's box. Not the right shape for a ring, she noted with a tiny trace of disappointment.

He took out a house key. What was that doing in a jeweler's box?

"Let's start with this." He pressed it lightly into her palm. "That's to my house. I know you don't want to live there while I'm still married to Esther, but I'd like you to come and go as you please. Bring Brady swimming. Cook in my kitchen. Hang around."

The point of this whole production was to give her a key to his house? Kate felt a twist of dismay. "Honestly!"

"Also, there's this." He tilted the box to reveal a gold chain with a pendant in the shape of a smaller key, sparkling with diamonds. "The key to my heart. I'll buy you a ring, of course, but it'll be a few months before we can get married. If you'll marry me. Will you, Kate?"

For some reason, the only words she could muster were, "Who says you aren't poetic?" Then she realized he was staring at her anxiously, as if the whole world hung in the balance. Which, indeed, it did. "Yes."

"That's yes you'll marry me?"

"Yes, I'll marry you, you crazy man."

When he kissed her, Kate got lost in the taste of him and the way his arms closed around her. *You outshine her in every way.... You and the kids are everything to me.* She would savor those words for the rest of her life.

A squeak from the rear seat recalled them to the present. Grinning, Tony escorted her and Tara inside and returned for their belongings. What a lot of stuff they'd brought home! Soon the living room overflowed with flowers, Kate's overnight bag, sample packages of disposable diapers and baby lotion, hospital discharge papers and, dropped on the coffee table, the surrogacy contract.

"I'll feed it through the shredder," Tony said as she curled on the sofa with a cup of tea he'd fixed in the microwave. Tara dozed contentedly in the family bassinet that had once sheltered Kate and Mary Beth. Tony had arranged for the Ellroys to drop it off on their way to church.

"Are you kidding? I'm saving the contract for Tara," she teased. "It's a priceless artifact."

"You already have a copy."

"I'm keeping that one for my own records." Catching his hesitant look, she added, "If you're worried that I'm going to use it against you someday, I'll shred it, I promise."

He sneaked a peek at Tara before replying. "If not for that agreement, she wouldn't be here. And we wouldn't be here together. Let's have it bronzed."

They both chuckled.

Tony took her hands gingerly, so as not to spill the tea. "Tell me again that you're going to marry me."

"I'll marry you ten times over."

"What made you fall in love with me? At the beginning anyway?"

She tried to figure that out. "I think it was cutting your hair."

He regarded her with surprise. "What did my hair have to do with anything?"

"I'm an expert on hair. I know exceptional quality when I see it." Setting the cup down, she nestled against him. "When did you first decide you loved me?"

"Yesterday."

Now, that *was* strange. "I didn't see you yesterday. What inspired you?"

"My brother."

Kate was torn between amusement and skepticism. "Leo?"

"He told me to marry you. And he was right." Tony looped his arm around her. "I hope it's okay with you if he's my best man. He was best man at my last wedding and that didn't turn out so well, but on Leo's behalf, I should point out that he thoroughly disliked the bride. And he's quite fond of you."

"What kind of wedding would you like?" she asked dreamily.

"The kind that lasts for the rest of your life."

"We'd have to eat an awful lot of cake," she pointed out. "And I might get tired of wearing the same dress for years and years."

"You can take it off at night," he promised.

Outside, Kate heard her son's and mother's voices, followed by a light tap at the door. Since neither she nor Tony was inclined to stir, she called, "Come in!"

A key jiggled in the lock, and Irene peered in. "Everybody decent?"

"And comfortable," Kate said.

Brady ran to her. "Look at what Uncle Ray gave me." He held up a toy airplane.

"May I see?" Tony examined it solemnly. "That's a fighter."

"It's an F-22 Raptor." As if he'd done it a thousand times, Brady climbed onto Tony's lap and began showing him the features.

Irene went to the bassinet and collected her granddaughter. She settled into an easy chair close to Kate, and the two women exchanged warm glances.

There was no way her mother could miss the happiness Kate felt radiating from her. She didn't have to say anything yet about their engagement. There was plenty of time to break the good news to the people she loved.

She planned to savor each word and each reaction. Perhaps by the time she finished informing the entire world, she'd believe it herself.

TONY'S COLLEAGUES expressed amazement when they learned that the attorney who was such a stickler for crossing t's and dotting i's had tossed aside the surrogacy contract. "I wish I'd taken bets," Jennifer told him the week after Tara's birth. "I'd be a wealthy woman."

"You'd have won my money for sure," he conceded.

Tony changed in other ways, too. The hospital seemed to get along fine without him taking home a pile of paperwork every weekend, he discovered. Instead, he barbecued outdoors, helped Brady sound out letters in storybooks and occasionally played pool with Leo, despite the guy's bad habit of winning.

In his spare time, Tony had a new hobby: watching Tara. He loved seeing her nurse as Kate crooned to her, or, on a blanket, waving her hands and arms in a manner that surely presaged Olympic-quality gymnastic skills. As the weeks passed, her cooing turned into words that to the uninitiated might sound like "goo ga," but to her daddy indicated she was already preparing to deliver a verdict from the bench.

Sometimes, as he held his daughter, he felt his sister's presence. It wasn't anything he could prove, just a shimmer of awareness that told him she was at peace, and that she forgave him.

As for Esther, the two of them signed their settlement agreement and submitted it to the court. In a few more months, he'd be free.

WHAT ON EARTH was Kate going to do about the photographs?

Although she wouldn't be moving to Tony's house until after the wedding, Kate started right away planning how to pack. Now, while waiting for him to drive her to her six-week checkup, she stood in the living room studying the framed photos on the end table.

The teddy bear covering Esther's image made her smile. But what about that shot of Quinn on his motorcycle, his face alive with excitement? Quinn had already died once, far too young. It seemed cruel to put away his image.

And I'd miss him.

She was still mulling the subject when Tony arrived. He'd insisted on taking off work, since Kate couldn't drive until receiving Dr. Rayburn's okay.

After greeting her at the door, he studied her thoughtfully. "Something's bothering you." Tony had developed a remarkable knack for reading her moods.

"It's silly." Kate picked up the diaper bag. "Let's put Tara in the car."

"There's nothing wrong with Brady, is there?" he persisted. "He's doing okay at school, right?"

"Absolutely." In fact, Tony's frequent bedtime reading had inspired her son to work harder at sounding out the alphabet, with the result that he could now read quite a few words for himself.

"Then what?"

No sense arguing that they'd be late, because they'd allowed extra time. "I was just wondering, after we're married, where I should put that photo." She pointed to the display.

"Much as I like the teddy bear, I don't think we need to keep Esther's image around, even covered up," Tony teased.

She smiled. "Not that one. I meant Quinn."

He glanced at the photo. "Aren't you keeping a scrapbook for Brady?"

Kate nodded.

"That's the perfect place for it," he said.

Between the pages of a book? How confining for her daredevil first love, yet it *was* a logical decision. Kate tried to ignore her twinge of disappointment.

At the medical center complex, Tony accompanied her and Tara into the maternity clinic. In contrast to the last few visits when her enlarged abdomen had reduced her pace to a waddle, Kate strode briskly to the check-in desk, and then to the elevator.

A couple of nurses paused to exclaim over the baby. The sight of their pink uniforms reminded Kate that not so long ago she'd expected to be starting classes soon. Now, with a newborn to care for and a wedding to plan, she'd decided to delay nursing school until fall. Thanks to Tony's help, she didn't have to return to the salon, either.

She would never set the world on fire like Esther. But the only fire she cared about was the one blazing in her fiancé's eyes.

Her good fortune was brought home in Dr. Rayburn's office when she noted a trace of sadness underlying nurse Lori Ross's cheerful manner. She had to be hurting over her recent breakup with Dr. Sellers. It was too bad that caring for younger siblings had soured Lori on having kids of her own.

"You're in good shape," the nurse said as she weighed Kate. "Just a few more pounds to go. You're still breast-feeding, right? That should help."

"She swims and works out, too," Tony added.

"At your pool? I'm envious. You've got such a gorgeous place." Despite the teasing note, her comment reminded Kate that Lori had planned to hold her wedding reception at Tony's house.

Well, maybe she and Jared would work things out. Stranger things had happened. *Some of them to me.*

In the examining room, Dr. Rayburn shook their hands. "How's our girl?" he asked, beaming at Tara.

"Passed her one-month checkup with flying colors," Tony said.

"Great. And how's Mom doing? Any soreness?"

"Happily, no," Kate said.

Dr. Rayburn ran down a list of possible complaints. Then, while Tony took the baby for a walk, the obstetrician examined Kate and pronounced her incision healed. The thin red line would soon fade, he advised, and her earlier blood tests had come back normal.

"I'm delighted at how things worked out for you and Tony," he said as he tapped his notes into the computer.

"I can't help feeling that Tara was meant to belong to both of us," Kate admitted.

The doctor helped her up from the examining table. "She's a blessing. That's what makes my job so rewarding."

Alone in the room as she dressed, Kate thought about how different her life had become from that day three months ago when she'd learned of Esther's departure. She'd gained a daughter *and* a man she loved beyond measure. He'd become a second father to Brady, too.

Tony popped in with the stroller. "I didn't mean to be gone so long, but I got to talking to another dad. His son was born just a few days before Tara."

"You wanted a son initially," Kate recalled, fastening her jeans. "You were looking forward to playing baseball."

"I can play with Brady. Tara might enjoy it, too, when she's older." He cleared his throat. "That reminds me. I've been thinking about what we discussed earlier."

She slipped on her shoes. "What's that?"

"Quinn's picture."

The name quivered through her. Trying for a neutral tone, she said, "Oh?"

Tony glanced at Tara, then back to Kate. "You'd like to keep his photo on display, or you wouldn't have mentioned it. And you know what? He gave us Brady, and he helped shape the person you've become. He deserves a place of honor, not being shut away in a scrapbook."

Relief surged through her. "Are you sure?"

"Yes, but on one condition."

Uh-oh. "What's that?"

"That you pitch the shot of Esther and me. I wouldn't want her to sneak out from behind teddy some dark night and give us all a fright."

"Tony!"

Kate was still smiling as they went out. In the waiting room, they reached the exit door at the same time as another couple with a baby.

Tony greeted the husband and introduced him. "This is Kirk, the dad I was telling you about."

Startled, Kate recognized his wife from the clinic waiting room. Rosemary, too, seemed surprised. After they explained that they'd met before, they let the fathers walk ahead with the strollers. Their voices drifted back as they discussed their favorite child-development Web sites.

The other mom handed over a card. "Here's my phone number. I'm setting up a new mothers' group. If you're interested, we'd love to have you join us."

"I'd like that." Kate made a mental note to call her tomorrow.

Rosemary gave a little cough. "If you don't mind my mentioning it, I thought you were a surrogate."

"Tony's wife left him. He started coaching me, and we fell in love." That summed it up, in Kate's opinion.

"How romantic!" Rosemary's eyes twinkled with delight. "Who could have imagined?"

"Certainly not me."

When she'd agreed to be a surrogate, she hadn't had a clue what she was letting herself in for, Kate could see now. How naive she'd been not to realize that plans rarely turned out the way you expected.

Sometimes, she mused as she reached the elevator and slipped her arm through Tony's, they turned out infinitely better.

* * * * *

Watch for the next book in the Safe Harbor Medical series—THE HOLIDAY TRIPLETS—coming in December 2010, only from Harlequin American Romance.

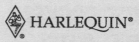

HARCNM0810

REQUEST YOUR FREE BOOKS!
2 FREE NOVELS PLUS 2 FREE GIFTS!

HARLEQUIN®

Love, Home & Happiness!

HARLEQUIN®

A *Romance*

FOR EVERY MOOD™

Spotlight on

Heart & Home

Heartwarming romances
where love can happen
right when you least expect it.

See the next page to enjoy a sneak peek
from Harlequin Superromance®,
a Heart and Home series.

Enjoy a sneak peek at fan favorite Molly O'Keefe's
Harlequin Superromance miniseries,
THE NOTORIOUS O'NEILLS, *with*
TYLER O'NEILL'S REDEMPTION,
available September 2010
only from Harlequin Superromance.

Police chief Juliette Tremblant recognized the shape of the man strolling down the street—in as calm and leisurely fashion as if it were the middle of the day rather than midnight. She slowed her car, convinced her eyes were playing tricks on her. It had been a long time since Tyler O'Neill had been seen in this town.

As she pulled to a stop at the curb, he turned toward her, and her heart about stopped.

"What the hell are you doing here, Tyler?"

"Well, if it isn't Juliette Tremblant." He made his way over to her, then leaned down so he could look her in the eye. He was close enough to touch.

Juliette was not, repeat, *not* going to touch Tyler O'Neill. Not with her fingers. Not with a ten-foot pole. There would be no touching. Which was too bad, since it was the only way she was ever going to convince herself the man standing in front of her—as rumpled and heart-stoppingly handsome now as he'd been at sixteen—was real.

And not a figment of all her furious revenge dreams.

"What are you doing back in Bonne Terre?" she asked.

"The manor is sitting empty," Tyler said and shrugged, as though his arriving out of the blue after ten years was casual. "Seems like someone should be watching over the family home."

"You?" She laughed at the very notion of him being here for any unselfish reason. "Please."

He stared at her for a second, then smiled. Her heart fluttered against her chest—a small mechanical bird powered by that smile.

"You're right." But that cryptic comment was all he offered.

Juliette bit her lip against the other questions.

Why did you go?

Why didn't you write? Call?

What did I do?

But what would be the point? Ten years of silence were all the answer she really needed.

She had sworn off feeling anything for this man long ago. Yet one look at him and all the old hurt and rage resurfaced as though they'd been waiting for the chance. That made her mad.

She put the car in gear, determined not to waste another minute thinking about Tyler O'Neill. "Have a good night, Tyler," she said, liking all the cool "go screw yourself" she managed to fit into those words.

It seems Juliette has an old score to settle with Tyler.
Pick up TYLER O'NEILL'S REDEMPTION
to see how he makes it up to her.
Available September 2010,
only from Harlequin Superromance.

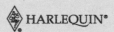

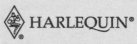

HARLEQUIN®

American ★ _Romance_®

TANYA MICHAELS
Texas Baby

Babies
&
Bachelors
USA

Instant parenthood is turning Addie Caine's life
upside down. Caring for her young nephew and
infant niece is rewarding—but exhausting! So when
a gorgeous man named Giff Baker starts a short-term
assignment at her office, Addie knows there's no time
for romance. Yet Giff seems to be in hot pursuit....
Is this part of his job, or can he really be falling
for her? And her chaotic, ready-made family!

**Available September 2010
wherever books are sold.**

"LOVE, HOME & HAPPINESS"

www.eHarlequin.com

HAR75325

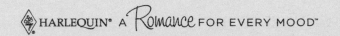